For Jonathan Strong

One

I slept three hours. I dreamed of Harry. It was the summer-vacation class annual show. We pantomimed to the *Chipmunks*. Harry was Alvin. Her brother Eddie was the director. It was exactly like our performance, except in the dream we wore black plastic wrap-around glasses.

I never experience a full night's sleep. After years of sleepless nights a slight nap's a full night's rest. Over time I tried everything to find a way to sleep. Drugs and alcohol. Meditation and yoga. Sex. Suddenly, I turned forty and started sleeping in two- and three-hour bursts. Four in the morning is the worst time, when I am most vulnerable to the racing thoughts and despicable anxiety; when I can levitate to a shaky hover.

I light a cigarette in the dark. My cup is

1

empty. At first light I will rise and steep more green tea. The heater blows invariably more than I need and I sleep in a sleeveless t-shirt with a sheet over me. Outside the temperature is below zero. Wind whistles through metal gutter pipes and rattles every creaky joint in the house. I rub my belly and test my flabby breasts to see if I want to masturbate. I rub my hair with my hand and smell my fingers. My dandruff is worse during the winter because of the excessive heat and dryness in my room. Mrs Hale has a habit of brushing the dandruff off my shoulder when she is speaking to me.

I snub out the cool menthol cigarette. All the different brands in nearly thirty years of smoking, I come back to the same brand Harry offered me behind the Curtis School when I smoked my first. It lifted me, and made me dizzy when I inhaled the way she showed me. Grandmother smelled smoke the moment I walked through the door. I told her some of the kids I played with were smoking. Denise said that was a lie and she saw me smoking with Harry and Billy Donovan.

I don't know how long it's been since Denise's last call. There's no way her new marriage will turn out better than any other, though this time she might get some money out of it. He left his wife, children and grandchildren. What kind of man would do that? At her age Denise is pushing it, there's no time left to be marketing herself as a young dish. She says he's sixty but thinks he's twenty-one.

They called Jim, Denise's father, Sully. He was attractive, in his own strange way, with blond hair and a beer belly. Sully was the dumbest of all Mother's men. He couldn't help me with sixth-grade arithmetic. No wonder he couldn't manage his business. Sully sells seashells by the seashore. Don't say that. Just did. Mother got rid of him after he lost his plumbing and heating business. He grabbed me. I slapped his face and he smiled. I told my mother she said don't be silly. Sully had an ex-wife and three other kids. I remember holidays when all the kids had to be together. I didn't like his children. I hid. He would find me and order me down to play with all my brothers and sisters. They're not my brothers and sisters.

Although I remain the Hales' house cleaner, after all these years, as Mrs Hale says, I'm like family. I've always felt some kind of barrier between me and Mrs Hale. Despite her ever-friendly gestures, she speaks to me in talk-down clips. The assumption is that I am her servant and couldn't possibly know as much as she does about anything. Dr Hale is all business, the good father and hard-working man of medicine.

I lost the rest of my customers during the last bout. The Hales remained supportive and welcomed me back. This stems in part from Mrs Hale's fear that she won't be able to replace me with another white person. I expect a call from Denise now that Grandmother is dead. As soon as she finds out, she'll want to know why nothing was left for her. It's really not much money, or a lot of money, depending on how I look at it. It's more than I've ever had at one time.

I'm glad I saw Grandmother in the end. I visited her a week before she died and she looked healthy as ever. She made beef stew. I helped her clean up the dishes. There was so much stew left she sent me home with it. I tried to tell her I didn't have a refrigerator only a tiny one-burner plate in my room. She said it would keep until the next day I should eat it then.

Harry said with no fear that God was in

people's minds. I see her spitting after she utters those words, then dragging on a cigarette. We roamed the neighborhood streets playing this way and that on our bikes. Harry showed me this way and that, a bike-riding game where you rode anywhere you wanted not paying attention to street signs until you ultimately found yourself outside the neighborhood in unfamiliar territory.

The day we rode to the Bear Hill Reservation out on the edge of town's when Harry told me about sex. I knew what she was going to say. Mother didn't make it a secret. But Harry told me the more important things, the girl things, and taught me about myself and my genitals and what was inside me. She already had done it with guys. She said she masturbated too. She told me what masturbation was and we pushed our bikes up Bear Hill and I had an idea what she was talking about because I was already having some of those feelings. When we were nearly to the top, we wheeled our bikes off the path for a cigarette. Harry started talking about sex again and what an orgasm was and did I ever have one? She fondled my breasts and then my vagina. Then she got on the ground and told me to get on top of her which I did, wrapping my legs around one of her legs as she pushed it up into me hard. I rode it looking out at cars below on Route 133, and the lights coming on in Wilton, a few of the old factories that were still making shoes lit-up.

We moved in with Grandmother when my father and mother broke up and they sold the house. He was the best she ever had, and caught her red-handed with another man. Mother got nothing out of the settlement but support for me because he never had as much as my mother suspected. My father was a hard-working man with a small construction company of his own. He specialized in reliable additions, roof repairs, fixing doors. No job too small. He loved her deeply, he told me so one day in tears when he picked me up and took me out for an ice cream. The divorce crushed him. In those days she was the kind of beauty that men stop dead on the street and stare at.

I met Harry the September I started in the Wilton schools. Mother said it was humiliating to have to move back to this shitty town. Everywhere she went people were talking. She started dating other men immediately. I don't remember any of them from that time. One day Harry and I were playing this way and that, we were over near Salem Street where there were a lot of bars and I saw Mother in a car in-between two guys in the front seat and they both had their arms around her. She didn't see me and I never said anything about it.

Mother wasn't around much and she was never awake in the morning before I left for school. My grandmother woke me and cooked eggs and toast or oatmeal which she called oakmeal. I don't remember Grandfather much. He was in the hospital when we moved back, stricken with cancer he died shortly thereafter. Before she was divorced my mother hardly brought us to visit, so my recollections of him are few. They lived in a two-story, single-family, tar-shingled, factory-worker house on Foster Street. It was one of the older neighborhoods, though when I was younger there was a small wooded area at the end of Foster where people dumped things. If I remember anything about my grandfather, it was his warning me to stay away from the woods because there were bad men living there.

In time, I saw my father less and less. It

wasn't because he didn't want to see me, but Mother made it very difficult for him. If he was going to come and pick me up she would take me out at the same time and later tell him he got the day wrong. Once he called the social services department to report her. They contacted my mother and she told them he was a drunk and she was afraid to let me get in the car with him. He tried to fight her but she just made things more tangled until he eventually moved away. But he never once missed a support payment for me. And he would call at night from Arkansas at prearranged times when we knew my mother would be out. Otherwise she would hang up on him.

In Arkansas he married another woman who Grandmother said was just like Mother. And he got divorced again, this time with a son, whom I never knew. He moved to California in the country somewhere where he could fish. We lost touch for years. Then he died from a heart attack. It was during the first time I was away. I didn't find out until I was released one month later. I wanted to fly out to California to visit his grave. I was in no condition.

The first time Harry and I skipped school we

took the train to Boston. Harry knew the subway system. She was afraid of us getting separated in the crowds, so she brought a pair of handcuffs and handcuffed us together. She showed me how to sneak into the subway under the turnstile when the man wasn't looking and we took the underground subway and above-ground trolley around various parts of the city and didn't get back home until late afternoon. The principal had phoned and spoke with my grandmother. She said she would not tell my mother this time. But I must promise her I wouldn't skip school again. It was one of many promises I never kept with her. Many a time she came between me and Mother who never could be rational under any circumstances. Mother just screamed and threw things and hit me with a broomstick.

For many years she worked a cocktail wait-ress, and I've heard other things too. She slept until noon and by the time I was arriving home from school she was readying to leave for work. If she had any free time she spent it with one of her boyfriends. She had no female friends to speak of. I helped Grandmother with the chores. I did laundry, cleaned floors and windows, changed bed-linen. Grandmother told me stories about her life in Ireland and how hard a man my grandfather was to live with.

I follow the exact system of cleaning I learned from Grandmother. It's much more efficient for me if Mrs Hale is out but once the cold weather sets in she's home permanently unless they take a ski vacation or fly to some place warm during the winter. When she's not there I can do the entire job inside of two hours by throwing a load of laundry in, starting downstairs in the kitchen and working my way out to the library, dining room, first-floor bathroom. Second floor is a huge family room with a big screen television. There's a guest bedroom, another bathroom and Mrs Hale's study which has some books and a computer she never uses. Third floor consists of the bedrooms, another bathroom and a master bathroom off the master bedroom. I vacuum, bed-change, back downstairs to throw the laundry in the dryer, back up to finish scrubbing the master-bedroom bowl.

Grandmother said those old things like clean house clean mind. A watched pot never boils.

It's a great life if you don't weaken. As long as you've got your health. She scrubbed and cleaned. She washed her walls and counters down with alcohol. When you hang a carpet out and give it a good beating you clean the carpet and clean out all the bad energy in your body. I never saw Mother make a bed. During the times she was married she had house cleaners or beds went unmade and unchanged.

Recently the Hales started a new cook. It's always the same. We love your food. Cook anything you like. That lasts about two weeks. They'll drive him out and be wanting me to fill in until they hire another one. It's not bad money to spend one day a week in the kitchen and put all this food up in the refrigerator and freezer. I can't really cook but I know what they want. I want out. I don't know what to do with Grandmother's money, but Dr Hale says it shouldn't be in a savings account where it is now and he can put me in touch with people and I can buy something called a Certificate of Deposit or mutual funds. I can do what I want now. Go to college again. Learn a trade. Anything but clean houses. I sit in the dark after a few hours' sleep and listen to the heat blow on and off.

Harry lived in one of the new side-by-side two-family houses which were called duplexes. They were built in the woods at the end of Foster Street. What was a mysterious forest when I was a child was barely enough area to contain the three duplexes with tiny back yards. The new homes looked out of place on Foster Street with its tar-shingled old factory-worker houses cramped every which way.

I was only inside Harry's house two or three times in all those years. I recall a startling quiet, and a clean that would have made Grandmother proud. Harry's parents were church-goers and active with various parish activities at Saint Ann's. Mr Harrington worked for the post office and Harry's older brother Eddie was known as a sissy. He had girlie mannerisms and didn't go in for sports like the other boys. Eddie looked a lot like Harry with his overbite and freckles. Though his hair was black and Harry's dirty blond.

They called her a tomboy. She was cute enough that the boys went for her. It frustrated them that she often made the best play of a

baseball game or ran for the winning touch-
down in tag-football. After we started hanging
out together I never went to church again. Her
parents went to the eight o'clock mass and we
met for the ten-fifteen. In the good weather we
rode our bikes around; in the bad weather we
hung out in a laundromat and smoked.

My mother never went to church and slept
through Sunday morning. Grandmother never
missed one week of confession or mass. She said
she didn't have many rules around the house
except that Denise and I go to confession, mass
and receive holy communion each week. Denise
continued to attend mass. She said in confession
she told the priests about all this made-up sex
stuff. And she enjoyed mass because there were
lots of boys to check out; she sat up front and
flirted with the altar boys. When Mother was
waitressing she worked Saturday nights. She
said she was too wound up to just come home
after her shift and stayed at the lounge for a
drink or two. Sometimes on Sunday morning
she wouldn't arrive home until after the sun had
come up.

Denise got Mother's looks and body. Tall,
thin, leggy and busty all in one. I had the great

body for about two years when I least understood it. Or, to put it another way, I had great
breasts before any of the other girls had them.
All the boys were friendly for a while and after
one thing. Tits drive boys crazy Harry said.
How do you figure they're just milk sacks.
Mother said I was fat and I would be fat all my
life if I didn't do something about it when I was
young. Grandmother said I was plump and had
a large frame, there was nothing I could do with
it, mine was an athletic body and that's the way
some girls were born.

Two

Harry was a year older than I was but she was kept back, so we were in the same grade. If she was in the mood she would go with a boy and let him have his way, although she said she liked playing sports with boys more than making out with them. Sometimes I let a boy feel me up. I humped Billy Donovan's leg and had an orgasm like I did the time with Harry.

Our make-out place was under the Route 133 overpass. We climbed a steep concrete-block grade and perched under the road in the steel rafters. The rumble of cars and trucks above resounding through the tunnel, and the occasional swish of cars from the rotary below, made us feel like we were in some out-of-this-world place. Sammy Carbone was the sweetest of all the boys. He liked to cuddle. We held each other close, gave each other soft kisses on the lips and he never tried to feel me up.

Harry went through the ice at Meadow Pond and people said any other girl would be dead. We all skated on Meadow Pond, and it froze solid each winter except at the far end where Corser Brook flowed in and the ice thinned out. Harry knew it, but she skated farther out than any of the kids, in black boys' hockey skates doing her foot-over-foot stride, dribbling a puck back and forth at the end of her stick, sound of blades carving the ice, splash and she's gone.

The Hale kids skate at a private skating club on an inside rink. One of Mrs Hale's chores is take the kids to their after-school activities. Sometimes she can't even do that and I've seen her put them in a taxi. Caroline takes cello lessons and plays soccer. Justin Jr plays football, baseball and basketball. Every hour after school is accounted for. Weekends it's the same. They plan family activities weeks, months, and years ahead, sitting around the table with a planner like they're running a business. When she's at home and functioning, Mrs Hale still checks my work when I'm finished, as if after all these years she'll catch me not cleaning one of the bathrooms, failing to vacuum a rug or leaving a load of laundry unfolded.

It's good to be home. To brew tea and open a can of soup. It's remarkably quiet down here and hard to tell that I'm in the city. These streets of Winterhill are so congested with two- and three-family homes, and most lots with large yards have long since been split up for rear dwellings. This house is an exception. In the summer I can walk back into the yard to look at the rows of flowers, vegetables and fruit trees that my landlords tend. My apartment is illegal. The Portuguese family who own the house finished off a room in the basement with a kitchenette and bathroom. I pay them cash every month. They speak little English and I no Portuguese, it makes it easy. The grandmother has a huge voice and shouts everything she says in rapid-fire action. They fight once or twice a day but the nights are quiet.

There are seldom phone messages, except maybe the Hales asking me to do something for them like pick up one of the kids or stop at the store on my way in tomorrow. Sometimes the phone rings but no one leaves a message. Mrs Hale said those calls are pesky salespeople. One man left a message. He was from a securities or financial office and said he needed to speak to me about my recent loss and the financial implications. It sounded official until I phoned and he was a financial advisor who wanted me to give him Grandmother's money to invest. He said he had some ideas that he knew would be beneficial to me and my family and when would be a convenient time to come out and discuss them with me. There are letters from insurance salesmen. And car salesmen. They read the obituaries for future clients. There is no good time.

I'd been without sleep for weeks when they finally admitted me the first time. It got to a point that when I slept, the nightmares were so bad it was as if my body was defending itself against itself and wouldn't allow me to sleep. But then the nightmares were coming while I was awake. Grandmother had no choice but to get help. She was a simple woman and didn't understand. It was Father Foley from Saint Ann's who told her to call the doctor. She thought maybe I needed to be exorcised. They said the ECT would help me forget. Grand-mother came every day to the hospital. She brought me books, magazines and flowers. I didn't even know who she was at first. I'm your grandmother.

She tried her best to teach me things about a woman's cycle and sex but she got embarrassed. She repeated something about a man has to plant the seed, and a woman is the earth. It was impossible to believe that she was my mother's mother they were so different. Harry told me everything. She had periods before I did. She made it sound like no big a deal except for the mess. Even now, there's something I like about the cramps and when they begin to come, I welcome them, as if my insides are telling me I am alive.

Harry passed out from sniffing glue and I thought she died. All the other kids ran. We were on the fire escape of the Curtis School on the top tier. I stayed with her and kept opening her eyelids and telling her not to die. It was just getting dark. Billy Donovan and the others ran out through the entrance at the far end of the schoolyard. I thought maybe I should run too but I couldn't leave her.

Mostly I sit in bed. I have no television or radio. As a child, I remember watching shows like *Leave it to Beaver* wondering where those families were and Denise said California that's where she was going to go some day and she did. Her first husband was a hot-shot hairdresser with a string of hair salons whom she met at a party. She moved to the West Coast two weeks later and married him. She'd done the suicide thing before, so it didn't surprise me all the shit she pulled when he ran off with someone else after he lost his salons. There never was a string, only two. Theirs was an open marriage, and the two of them were swapping partners. I don't know what she expected.

The cramps are getting worse. I'm about to start flowing any minute. My periods are more intense as I get older. I light a cigarette and finish my cup of tea. The woman upstairs is shouting at her granddaughter. It's four of them living there. I don't know where the child's father is, I've never seen him.

My mother grudgingly ate Sunday dinner with us. Grandmother insisted that on Sunday anyone in her home must sit down and eat. She called upstairs several times for Mother, who might be getting out of bed into the shower, we're waiting and dinner's getting cold. Even when she was there it was as if she were not, though she was always charming, calling us her sweet things or dear ones and patting us on the head. Before dinner was finished she lit a cigarette, made phone calls, and shortly thereafter she disappeared for the day, and that was the most we saw of her in a week.

Grandmother lost four pregnancies after she gave birth to Mother. She said that if Mother wasn't an only child she might have grown up to be a different person. After my mother divorced Denise's father we moved back in with Grandmother again. My mother didn't spend much time in Wilton. Most of her waitress jobs were in Brockton and for a while she drove all the way to Boston every night. Grandmother forbade her to smoke pot in the house but she paid her no mind and sometimes if I woke to go to the bathroom after she got home I could smell it coming from her room. Grandmother got up after mother fell asleep to look and see she didn't leave a cigarette burning on the bed.

The furnace is directly next to my room. First there is click and the sound of the machine firing-up. Then a pause. Then the blower kicks in. Even with my vent closed I get too much heat because it has so little area to travel. It's so dry my scalp flakes. I rub my head and smell it with other people around but mostly I have that under control. I rarely do the blinking thing with my eyes any more. The heat blows. Upstairs is quiet they must be in bed. Because my heating vent is closed the air forcing through it whistles.

We attended vacation school at Saint Ann's during the month of July. It was a chance for the nuns and priests to indoctrinate public school kids. There were snacks and games, an annual talent show and a trip to Washburn Lake Amusement Park. Mostly we read catechism, sang religious songs, listened to the nuns and priests tell us about Christ and original sin. They showed us movies and slide movies. I remember spikes through his hands, how he was made to hang there.

One year at Washburn Lake Harry and I rode the roller coaster all day. As soon as we finished a run, we went straight back into the line, the longest line in the park. By the end of the day we rode that coaster sixteen times, front car, back car, middle car. Every single ride Harry held her hands over her head and never touched the safety bar. I got sick on the bus ride home and was forced to ride with my head between my legs, throwing up into a bag. All the while Harry sat next to me and rubbed my back and neck.

Her real name was Kathleen Harrington. She blew great smoke rings and freely talked about sex, or her vagina and its workings, like it was perfectly natural. Grandmother referred to her as that Harrington girl. Though Grandmother rarely spoke ill of anyone, in the early days she frequently hinted that I might do well to associate with other kinds of girls too. Regarding Denise Grandmother would only say that she never had a chance like I did. What she meant was that at least I had Grandmother. Denise really never had anyone. She could have had Grandmother; instead she saw her as the enemy.

That's the way it is with Denise. You are either with her or against her. Her great ally or her enemy. No middle ground. I've been on both sides. Denise hated Harry. She made up stories about her and spread them around. She made fun of Harry's brother Eddie and called him Edwina the Ballerina. By the time she was ten she had boys fighting over her. If the attention on her waned, she created a crisis and everyone came running. Mother indulged her when she was around. Grandmother ignored her. I often did a little of both. But the older we grew I tended to side with Grandmother.

I call up a dream while I am awake. It's as if I dreamed that very dream last sleep. But the more I examine the dream, my vivid recollection dissolves into variations of a dream I've dreamed hundreds of times. Or maybe just once. There's a house and Harry and I are cleaning. We're climbing stairs. Harry is talking. She's talking fast jumping from one subject to the next, as she could, ahead of me on the stairs. She reaches the fourth level and says oh my this is what always happens I told them we hadn't cleaned yet. I reach the top floor. Mr and Mrs Hale, Caroline, the baby and Junior. Blood's splattered everywhere. Harry picks up one of those medieval handles with the spiked ball on the end which has been sitting on the floor. Now I know where this is. She begins to clean as if everything's normal. The Hales are strewn all about the room their faces and skulls bashed in. The carpets, floors, walls and ceiling are soaked with blood. Harry what are you doing? Harry?

A thin beam of light seeps in from outside. The streetlamp light streams from the head of the driveway, down through the narrow space between the closed window shade and the window casing, and into my room. Without that light there would be a fainter light from somewhere. Without the furnace there would be sound from elsewhere. There is always light somewhere. There are always sounds.

Three

Summers we swam in Corser Brook. There was a small beach at Meadow Pond but we walked a woods path to where the railroad bridge crossed over a deep pool. We jumped off the bridge. Harry and I swam by moonlight. She took off all her clothes but I was afraid the police might come and I might be seen naked. I jumped feet first but Harry dove straight off, even at night she plunged to the pool's depths and came up with a rock to prove she'd been to the bottom. She'd play tricks and swim underwater to the other side of the bridge and, while I stood overhead screaming, she'd sneak up on me from behind with a boo.

I weighed one hundred and eighty-five pounds by the time I was twenty. I wore potato-sack dresses or overalls. I hated looking at myself in the mirror and had none in my room. I cut off all my hair like a boy so I could just let it dry after showering and not have to tend to it. Grandmother said it was a shame because my full wavy hair was one of my best features. I ate lots of food. I wasn't partial to anything special. Cakes, chips, pizza, French fries, peanut-butter and jelly sandwiches. I'd eat until I passed out then the dreams would start. Grandmother could only indulge me. She baked pies and cooked big dinners and brought things to my room and tried to make conversation. I didn't go out or see anyone.

In terms of age, Grandmother could pass for my mother. She gave birth to my mother when she was seventeen. My mother had me when she was sixteen. Grandmother was fond of singing, and I remember the first time we moved in with her and she sensed that I was scared, she baked special cookies and sang me to sleep. It was a song about fish having to swim and birds having to fly. When I was twenty she was only fifty-three.

A message came in at midnight. It's Denise, clueless to the time difference between here and California. She says hi it's me we need to talk about some things give me a call. With all the money that's been through her fingers she's after Grandmother's paltry savings even with her current husband who owns a private plane. I'll give her the money. I'm sure she has no idea what a nominal amount it is. Neither did Grandmother. You'll get it all, she often said with a tone that made it sound like she was leaving me a huge estate. It's not that I'm ungrateful. Between working, welfare, and Medicaid, I've done all right over the years and never taken from her except for a place to stay when I couldn't get one myself. The house needed a lot of work and property in Wilton isn't exactly prime. She had a life insurance policy she paid month in month out, going back to the days when the insurance man would come to the door and collect the money. The policy barely covered the cost of her funeral. I buried her next to Grandfather at the Wilton Memorial.

It's been years since I shaved any part of my body. I twirl the hair under my left armpit with my right fingers. My fingers smell of my body. I rub my scalp with my right hand, hard so that it almost hurts, flakes fly up in a dust-storm around me. I twirl my hair again. My fingers smell of the earth. I place my right pinkie finger into my right ear and rotate it around. Earth and potatoes. My left hand is for cigarettes. Between my first and second finger there's a brown stain. The smell of burned tobacco never goes away even when I wash my hands. My left hand is smoke. My right hand is my body. I sit up and rub my hands over my belly. I squeeze the belly fat hard between both of my hands.

I never went back to the Urich house after the incident over the missing money. Four years of service and the first sign that some cash was missing they blamed me. Professor Urich, the big lecturer at Harvard and author of a famous book, the great humanitarian, groveling on the phone to me how sorry he and his wife were, how badly they felt about their mistake and how much they liked me and wanted to keep me on as their cleaner.

Sully always had beer on his breath. He and my mother were nearly broke up when he cornered me those few times. It was kind of pitiful. I was never afraid of him. Wild fights erupted between them at any time. Sometimes they would continue for hours, especially if they were both drunk. Mother would scream through the night at the top of her lungs. Get the fuck out of here. I hate your fucking guts. She slammed doors and threw things. All the neighbors could hear. Sully never got loud or violent, he responded in a quiet voice. I'm not going anywhere. I'm staying right here. And he sat in his recliner silent drinking beer which was his way of taunting her. Sometimes she would jump on him, scratch and punch in order to provoke a response. The most he would do was stand up, wrap his arms around her waist, lift her up and carry her to the bedroom. He'd put her down and walk out closing the door behind him. She followed him out and immediately started over again.

When neighbors called the police, Mother claimed that Sully was beating her up and she wanted him out. Sully remained inert in his recliner. I haven't touched her ask the kid. I had to stay in my bedroom but I could hear everything. The police would remain a few minutes and talk with each of them separately, then together. After they left Mother and Sully would wander off to bed and I would sit in the dark and listen to them. First the giggling, then the laughing, then Sully groaning a low slow oh yeah and mother screeching her high-pitched ahhhhh-yia, their bed rocking the house until they eventually passed out and everything went quiet.

The tide is going out. Harry is swimming hard and fast with those determined strokes of hers and her head turning in time, her feet paddling like a machine. Harry don't go out too far. It's rainy and cold, not beach weather. She stops now, treading water way out there. She raises one of her arms up in the air and shouts but I can't hear her over the sound of the surf and the wind. She rolls over and begins to swim again, farther out with the tide. Harry cut it out and come back. Farther out. Harry cut it out.

Four

First there is bright light. Second there is a shadow. Third there is a sound.

Then there is absolute blankness.

Then, slowly, a terror of not knowing who I am or what is happening overcomes me.

The shadow gradually takes on features. The sound develops into a voice which slowly clarifies from an electronic muddle to words.

You are Laurel Bell. You are at the South Shore Mental Health Center. You have just had a treatment.

I am confused and scared.

Do you understand what I am saying? You are Laurel Bell. You are at the South Shore Medical Center. You have just had a treatment.

Gradually the fragmented associations click in. I am told my name again. Where I am again. What is going on again. Why I am here again.

They have always been good to me, the nurses and doctors. It's rough in there. People get hurt and it's more likely to be a staff member than a patient. I wonder what they think when they see those of us they recognize, the ones who return dependable as the seasons.

There are so many varieties of green tea, I have yet to sample them all. The furnace is blowing. I snub out a cigarette. I am horny. I'm afraid that's not a good sign. I'm afraid when I begin to feel. The thinking part I can cope with; the feeling part's where I find myself adrift.

Harry said waking after passing out from glue was the same as waking the time she went unconscious going through the ice. On glue she was only out for a minute or two. No sooner did the wave of panic sweep over me, she was coming to and trying to lift her head up. But when she went through the ice they had to resuscitate her, and if she was under the water any longer, they say she could have suffered brain damage.

First she said was light. Then shadows. Then voices. Then confusion. The confusion might last for days. I'm clumsy. Every action feels awkward to perform. I knock things over. Even walking is difficult. My short-term memory is practically non-existent. I could wander off the unit so they watch me and follow me around. Then, just as the particles begin to settle, another session. And it begins all over again. Three per week. Three weeks in a row. It helps me forget.

My mother used all her various last names as it convenienced her. She was Lisa Clark. Lisa Bell. Lisa Sullivan. Baby Jennifer was said to be a La Valley but it was never proven. Mother never married Ray but she used his last name for a while too. Lisa La Valley she said has a lot of class. Denise, like mother, has a string of last names. She was born Denise Sullivan. Then she married Bobby her first husband and became Del Grecco. Her second husband was a Peterson and now her third Grassfield. There was nearly a fourth marriage wedged somewhere in there. It was called off after some kind of crisis that Denise caused. I don't remember the details, she was in California and I was in the hospital.

It took me by surprise when I phoned her and she didn't mention anything about Grandmother's money going to her. She said she was glad I had something of my own and she didn't have to worry about me now. Her pregnancy was the big news. I love him, I really love him. Her new house was huge and from her kitchen window she had a view of the mountains. I've never been so happy. The previous day they flew in his plane and watched the sunset from the air. Isn't that the most romantic thing you ever heard? And she went on like that for fifteen minutes completely uninterrupted, talking away, going through a list of the most minute details of the day-to-day things she and her new husband had been doing. And what a tiger in bed. You'd never know he's sixty. Her pregnancy can only mean this guy's got more money than she ever dreamed. I listened. I congratulated her. I must listen. If she asks me a question, by the time I'm half-way through with an answer, she interrupts to talk about herself again.

A sleepless night isn't worrisome to me any longer. I seldom have two in a row. Lying still in the dark, even without sleep, allows the body some rest. I don't find Dr Hale attractive, but his passivity and boyishness can be appealing. I imagine him a rambunctious lover, a kid jumping into a haystack, though from what I gather from Mrs Hale there's not much going on between them at this time. Once I was in the basement and heard Mrs Hale confiding to her sister on the phone that she was never able to enjoy it, not the way you do she said.

Sully tried to be a good father to Denise, stepfather to me and father to his other children. One afternoon he gathered all of us in the back of his truck and drove us to where he rented a pony for the afternoon. He led each of us around on the pony, then took us for hamburgers. Another time we took a hike up Bear Hill. When we got to the top, he pulled a can of beer from his pocket and drank it down in a few gulps. Mother never came along on such adventures. When she and Sully went to Bermuda for a week they left me and Denise with Grandmother. Mother never took us on any of her tropical vacations. What kind of vacation would it be with the two of you tagging along.

Sully's company contracted with the town of Brockton. He had plenty of work and employed a crew of men. Then there was a scandal concurring bribes and politicians. Sully was somehow involved and he lost his contracts.

Instead of going out and generating new business, Sully laid off most of his crew. Then he sold all the vans with the fancy lettering Sully's Plumbing and Heating except one. He started drinking more and working less. The fights got worse and my mother was trying to get him to move out of the house but he wouldn't budge. She had a sense that the money was running out. She also had a growing fear that Sully was draining his company of money, and diverting it so that she wouldn't be able to get at it legally. Sully never did pay mother child support for Denise. At least none that Mother admitted to.

I remember my father took me to his place for the weekend. I got sick at his apartment and threw up all over myself. I was four or five. I was terrified because I had no control over my bodily functions. Father kept cleaning me up and carrying me to the bath wrapped in a towel to wash me off with warm water. Everything's going to be OK. Everything's going to be OK. He had an old cushiony chair and we spent most of the weekend snuggled in it watching television, Father with his arms wrapped around me.

Billy Donovan was the cutest kid in the

neighborhood. Even if he was a little short. He had blond hair, blue eyes, a sincere and spontaneous smile. I didn't let on to Harry at the time, but it crushed me when she told me. Billy seemed so innocent and Harry said he was until she got hold of him. He had eleven brothers and sisters. His parents came from Ireland and I had a hard time understanding either of them when they spoke. Grandmother said they came from a different part of Ireland than her parents did. I never openly flirted, but I tried to be near him whenever I could. Sometimes we walked home together. His house was directly behind ours and he liked to cut through our backyard.

I'm at my mother's apartment and it's me and Denise, Harry, Mother, baby Jennifer and a man who I can't identify, though in the dream I'm familiar enough to converse with him. We hear giggling from the porch. I rush to the window and look out. Someone is out there. The man runs out and catches Billy Donovan and several of his brothers spying in the window. He drags them into the apartment by the necks of their shirts. Billy says they have gifts they wanted to bring and he pulls out a gift-wrapped box and hands it to me. I undo several layers of wrapping down to a cardboard box. Inside the box is a blue glass bell. I lift the bell out of the box. It has no ringer. Billy says ringers are bad luck and can turn glass to blood.

Billy made out with me. I let him feel me up and he let me hump his leg but for a long time I was afraid to do anything more. I liked Billy more than any other boy. Harry said I wanted someone with a little experience, otherwise you might not know if it's right or wrong. I understood where he was going to put it, but I was horrified that it might hurt and I would bleed everywhere. You have to be relaxed about it, otherwise you won't be able to enjoy it she said.

Mrs Serge reminds me of Grandmother. Physically they are much different. Mrs Serge is tall, muscular and worldly. During the late summer she knows which of the mushrooms growing on the Hales' lawn are safe to eat. She knows about poetry and politics, art and music. The Hales won't eat any of the mushrooms so she fills up her basket before she leaves for home. She's great with the children, especially

Eliza. Mrs Hale says the other two combined were easier than Eliza.

I don't understand how someone like Mrs Serge, who in her homeland was a music professor, would have to take work as a baby-sitter here in this country. It's her passion for living and for people I envy. When neither of the Hales are home, she sits at the their piano and plays. She knows hundreds of pieces by memory. I sit in the living room and listen. She enjoys the audience. There's something about the way the notes can cut right through me. Without words. The pitch and fall of sound.

Five

For several years you never saw one of us without the other. We didn't have to make phone calls or prearrange meetings. I knew where Harry would be at a given time or she knew where I would be. We shared everything; and Harry not only knew about sex, but she could talk about places in the world as if she'd been there herself. Tropical countries. Frozen continents. Far away cities. I thought she made things up, the way she would come out of nowhere in the middle of a conversation about cats she'd say in China they eat cats. Are you making that up? You're making that up. I'm not making it up it's true.

Sleety-snow whips against the windows and vinyl siding, hard enough to be heard over the furnace. The room brightens up for an instant as I flick the lighter and the flame ignites the tip of my cigarette. Dark again. A long drag on the cigarette. A soft red glow over the white bed sheet. I keep the clock turned around on the dresser. It doesn't matter what time it is. The habit began years ago when I couldn't sleep. It helps not knowing what time it is. Sometimes when I get up for a bathroom run I'll turn it around and peek. The tea makes me pee. Sometimes it's within a minute or two of my guess. Other times I'm hours off.

A light. A shadow. A voice. The gradual awakening back into some kind of conscious being. Memory lifts off. Particles rustle and get caught up in the air currents. Clouds form and turn in and out on themselves, amorphous, but gathering energy and force as they go. Something has to give. Blank sky and no footing.

Betsy Milmoe said something about Harry. Harry said something about Betsy Milmoe. For a week everybody said there was going to be a fight. Betsy was bigger and older than Harry. She was crass and loud, always pushing girls and boys around. It was a hot summer afternoon. I saw Betsy walking through the entrance of Dilboy Park. Harry looked up and saw her too. She took one last drag on her cigarette, threw it on the ground and stamped it out hard with her sneaker.

Betsy had five or six kids with her. We had about the same. Betsy said I hear you've been saying some things about me, Harrington. Harry said maybe I have but what goes around comes around. Betsy said if you're not ready to say you're sorry you better be ready to get your ass kicked. Harry said I don't want to fight you Betsy, but if I have to I will. Hit her Betsy her friends shouted. Harry's brother Eddie broke in and told Betsy nobody wanted any trouble. Betsy said fuck off you sissy. Eddie said fuck you Betsy and got ready to stand his ground but Harry pushed him out of the way and told him she could handle her own battles.

When Billy Donovan fought Charley Dunn bloody, it bothered me a lot, but I figured that's what boys did. But to see Harry and Betsy in the ninety-degree heat, swapping punches, wrestling each other to the ground, clawing, biting, kicking. I couldn't get it out of my mind for days. But two girls. Harry was much quicker and each time she punched Betsy in the face, a bruise rose on Betsy's cheek or forehead or chin. Betsy pulled out a handful of Harry's hair. Kids were yelling and worked up into a fury. I was horrified and became sick to my stomach. As much as I hated Betsy Milmoe, I felt for her every time Harry bought a fresh welt to her face. Finally, a man pulled over and got out of his car, took one look at the two girls and got between them. By then they were so exhausted they gratefully accommodated the man's demand to break it up immediately. Betsy's friends said it was a draw. Considering Harry was smaller and younger, we figured she got the best of it. Her face and arms were scratched and bleeding. There was a white mark on her scalp where Betsy pulled the hair out.

Grandmother told me by the time my mother was thirteen she had no control over her, just like with Denise. Mother came and went as she pleased. There were nights that she didn't come home. Grandfather was of the old school and did things like lock her out. Mother told me that he used to hit her too. Grandmother was drawn into the middle having to protect my mother, while knowing at the same time that my mother needed some kind of limits set on her.

The first time my mother got pregnant she

was fifteen. She had an abortion. Grandfather never knew. Grandmother gave her the money behind his back and assisted in finding a safe place to have the procedure performed. Grandmother didn't believe in abortion. But she was afraid for mother who refused to disclose the identity of the baby's father. She feared my grandfather and his reaction. When he lost control he was capable of crazy behavior. Mother told us Grandfather used to beat Grandmother. Grandmother said she only remembered a slap once or twice. Briefly, Grandmother contemplated sending Mother off somewhere to give the baby to a Catholic organization. Mother told her there was no way she would have the baby and then give it up. Wilton was a smaller place back then Grandmother said. One year later Mother was pregnant again but she miscarried.

Mrs Hale had a breakdown after Eliza was born. It looked like a breakdown; except Mrs Hale remained home instead of being hospitalized. There were private nurses there around the clock, taking care of her and the baby. Dr Margolis, an old family friend, looked in on

Mrs Hale once a day and had her heavily medicated.

Every reference of Mrs Hale to Eliza is couched in her animosity. Everything was fine until Eliza came. I never got sick during pregnancy until Eliza. Things have not been the same between me and James since Eliza. It's strange how people will say most anything in front of servants, as if they're not there. Mrs Hale has a way of softly purring and pawing her way around, doing very little while at the same time appearing to be the perfectly competent doctor's wife, vulnerable, mousy and non-threatening.

The Hales produce so much dirty laundry that the washer and dryer run continually while I am there. The last thing I do before I am finished for the day is fold the clean clothes and pile them high in baskets on the basement floor. There are dozens of pairs of socks to sort and match. Mr and Mrs Hale's underwear. Sports uniforms. The kids' clothes. Jeans and slacks. Sweaters, shirts, baby clothes, bibs, table-cloths, napkins, towels, bed sheets, bedspreads, pillow-cases. Mrs Hale's blouses and skirts with her special washing instructions so that I have to do them all separately. Sweatshirts, sweat pants, Dr Hale's golf and tennis clothes.

When I learned to do laundry with Grandmother, we washed by hand in her big oversized sink using a washboard and brush. Even after she got an electric washer, she never wanted a dryer. Everything was hung out on the long clothesline that extended from her back door high to a big oak tree that stood in the rear of the yard. The pulleys were rusted and let out metallic squeals as she ran another strip of wet hanging clothes over the yard. In the winter she had rope lines in the basement near the furnace where the clothes dried quickly and shriveled.

As the days grow longer more light seeps in through the narrow basement window. The shade is drawn but light emanates around the edges so by daybreak, various objects in the room gather out of the darkness. My dresser. A pile of clothes on the floor. Grandmother's chest at the foot of my bed, the top of which resembles the round top of a gravestone. The telephone on the little table. The corner chair. It must have snowed even though spring is near. The landlord is shoveling, his shovel-blade is scooping and scraping outside the window.

Upstairs the little girl is jumping around from room to room. Her grandmother is shouting at her. Then the girl's mother begins arguing with her mother in Portuguese. Grandmother shouts her down.

Six

School work came easy for me. My grades were good and my efforts minimal. Reading and writing I liked most, and competing in a spelling Bee I was a finalist every time. When I took the exam for my high-school general equivalency test I passed effortlessly. Grandmother encouraged me to go to college. You're a smart girl. There's no reason you can't do anything you want to do.

I don't read. I don't write. I don't like to add up how many hours I worked for the Hales. I'd be unaware if they try to beat me for an hour or two each week. I don't want to clean the Hales' house any longer. I don't want to change baby Eliza for Mrs Hale when Mrs Serge is not around. It's always the same with Mrs Hale. Can you do me a quick favor and change the baby I've got to run upstairs and do something?

Grandmother took us to the hospital when Jennifer was born. Because the birth was premature they put Jennifer in an incubator. She was a tiny, wrinkly thing and resembled a laboratory specimen under glass. Mother looked great with her face made-up and her hair brushed out. She kept sneaking into the bathroom to smoke.

Grandmother and I mostly took care of Jennifer. Mother worked late, slept late, held the baby for about five minutes over her cup of black coffee and the day's first cigarette. She bounced Jennifer on her knee until the first sign of any discomfort on Jennifer's part, then she handed her off to me or Grandmother. Denise wanted nothing to do with Jennifer. Suddenly, Denise was no longer the baby. I fed Jennifer, changed her, held her when she cried and listened to Grandmother for tips on what to do and what not to do like make sure you clean her thoroughly inside her private area, as Grandmother called it. In the first days I watched her eyes start to focus. Then she was able to hold her head up. She made near-silent coos, sighs. In the middle of the night, she cried so fearfully,

Grandmother's touch was the only one that brought her relief.

I didn't fit in with the kids at school. The popular boys and girls walked to school with crowds around them. If I wasn't walking with Harry I walked alone, or if I felt particularly brave, on the outskirts of one of the circles. Billy Donovan could hang out with the most popular group and then hang out with me and Harry. I didn't have the cheerleader glow like a lot of girls; and I resented them for it. In high school Harry and I were in different classes. We met in the third-floor girls' room after second period for a cigarette, and also in the courtyard after fifth period. I can see her standing outside the Building C door, drenched without a hat or rain jacket, smoking a Salem.

The first time I tried pot with her was on the hill behind the high school. Harry said she liked it better than glue or beer. She showed me how to hold the joint and draw in the smoke. It made me choke and I coughed wildly but nothing happened. The second time I tried was on the same hill during the winter. We shared a joint and I was still convinced that nothing happened. Walking down the hill, I began to feel powerful rushes swelling up through my body, I could almost hear them and they swished out through my ears. I was confused and my heart was beating fast. I slipped on the snow and slid all the way down the hill, by the time I got to the bottom I was laughing so uncontrollably my nose was running down my face. At home Grandmother wanted to know what was wrong with my eyes because they were red. I don't remember what I told her, but I ate voraciously then went directly to bed.

That was the last time I smoked pot until I was older when I found it made me paranoid, more depressed, and hungry. Harry said smoking relaxed her and made her feel part of everything. Mother said that too. I should have known why people were showing up at the house for quick visits. And all the phone calls, younger neighborhood kids too – including Harry.

With her bathroom cabinet overflowing with pill bottles, Mrs Hale goes on tirades about drugs. She says if they could just get rid of drugs there would be so much less trouble in the world. Sometimes, just when I start to feel better is when I play with the dosages, or stop taking my medications. But after all these years I've learned that the longer I manage to stay on the proper dosage, the longer I go without major trouble. Denise started doing cocaine when she was young. It's the reason her first husband lost his hair salons.

I've missed so many years. There were treatments. I was in and out of the hospital and recovering at Grandmother's. I don't know how she managed during that time. Grandmother kept things inside. She never voluntarily spoke about anything unless I brought it up first. We must put it behind us so we can heal. Nothing we say can change a thing.

A light. A shadow. A voice. The heater switches off. It must be midday and sunny judging by the amount of light stealing in. Shouts of school children from the nearby elementary school. The regular bang of metal to metal from somewhere. Every few minutes a plane taking off or landing from the Boston Airport. They say when the wind blows a certain way they route the planes over Winter-hill. Then the song of birds.

The first time Harry ran away from home she lived in the loft of a barn in Bobby Burke's back yard. At dark she came out to hang with us behind the Curtis School. Another time she ran she hitchhiked to Boston and we didn't hear anything for a week until the authorities found her and she was returned. Her reasons for running were vague. If I asked her why she ran she said oh I'm just not going to put up with their crap any more and dismiss it with a hand gesture. She never suggested anything wrong was going on at home and she seemed to have more freedom than any other kid, coming and going as she pleased. I never got to talk with Eddie about anything after it happened. We never spoke another word to each other before the Harringtons sold their house and moved away.

No sooner I was getting into boys, Harry was losing interest in them. Billy Donovan was sensational, for about a minute. Before I even figured out what was going on it was over. We made out, rolled around in Bobby Burke's loft, and I knew it was time. I liked how our touching made me feel. And I liked Billy. He tried to unsnap my jeans but he couldn't. I was self-conscious that I was too fat and my jeans too tight so I slipped over and unfastened them myself. Billy lifted my legs in the air and pulled my jeans over them. I forgot about my sneakers, so Billy just pulled them off without unlacing them. He said he had a rubber and removed one from his pants' pocket. Then he dropped his pants and underwear at the same time and Billy looked at my legs and I thought he must think they're too fat. He got down beside me and we tried to pick up where we left off but this time he was in a hurry to get the rubber on and get inside me. I wanted him to kiss me, but he sucked on one of my breasts so hard I told him to go easy it hurt. Then it was over.

I didn't know what to make of it. If that was it, then why did everyone act like it was such a big deal? Harry said that's the way it was with boys. She asked me did I have an orgasm and I didn't. She kissed me on the cheek and hugged me. Said she loved me, I was her best friend ever. There were other feelings she had for me too. Harry I said I'm not like that.

Seven

I've had two relationships that lasted longer than one month. Aaron and I made it six months, though it was doomed from the beginning since he was my therapist. Nancy and I were together for eight months. It might have been longer but she left me. Who wants to spend their life with someone who mopes around depressed all of the time. She knew about me when we moved in together, but she thought she could change me. I want to make it better for you she said. Nancy did make life better for me. But she wanted to make it better for me on her terms.

Aaron drank. After we became involved, he suggested I get a new therapist, which I did. Ours wasn't as much a physical relationship, though we had good sex the first month; but Aaron wanted someone who needed him, and wouldn't mind when he came home late from drinking after a long day of his sorting through other people's dirty laundry. I needed someone who wouldn't mind if they found me in the evening the same way they left me in the morning, in bed. Aaron understood me more than any other person I've known, including my grandmother. He came home slurring his words and tottering, dropped his clothes beside the bed and jumped in like an overgrown boy with a wide smile. I was awake and we embraced. Tell me how you are. And I told him how I was feeling while he stared at me with his blue eyes flaming red, nodding his head compassionately to my every word. When I finished, we shut the light, held each other in the dark until he began to snore loudly and I kept my arms wrapped tight around him.

Mrs Hale says I could be an attractive woman if I lost a little weight and did something with my hair and dress. She refers to my outfits as work clothes although by now she knows the corduroys, jeans, sweatshirts and t-shirts I wear in work or out. She loves shoes. Shoes are always on sale and there is always a good reason to buy a new pair. There is a closet off the master bedroom just for her shoes. Her dresses, like her shoes, demonstrate no individual taste. Dozens of slight variations on the same theme. Old-time standard patterns and colors. Plaids, florals, pastels. Her evening dresses, like her expensive blouses and skirts, are dry cleaned. I handle that too, making sure the cleaners follow Mrs Hale's specific instructions and seeing to her list of what night she'll need which outfit. Dr Hale is always giving or receiving some kind of award or attending a dinner with a board member from the hospital. The Hales even dine with the cardinal himself once a year, their social schedule is filled months in advance.

Grandmother wore the same blue knee-length dress every day. Once a week she washed it out and hung it to dry overnight. She wore simple black shoes and a blue and white check apron from the time she dressed in the morning until she undressed at night. Mother said it was a waste of money trying to buy nice clothes for me because I wouldn't wear them; and even if I did, I wouldn't look good in them. One of the few times I remember being dressed up was when I made my first holy communion in a white bridal-like dress with a veil. I had my picture taken holding an open catechism and the rosary beads in my hands. The photographer touched up the photo so I had this unnatural rosy glow about my cheeks. Grandmother brought me to Flora the hairdresser and she put my hair up in big rollers and I sat under the dryer. When Flora took out the rollers my hair was fluffier and curlier than usual for the entire afternoon.

In a city like Winterhill it's easy to remain anonymous because it is so congested with recent immigrants, students, and blue-collar families. I continued to live in Wilton for years. I tried going back to the high school. But the eyes were upon me everywhere I went. In school, on the street, in the supermarket. In time, the event diminished in the public's consciousness. At first there were newspaper articles and news spots, one year ago today, five years ago today; but there are too many other stories, even in a place like Wilton.

After I found my way out of Wilton, I began to understand what it was like to walk down the street or into a store or coffee shop without anyone having a clue about my past. To be able to look into the eyes of a clerk or a waitress, stand at a bus stop or in line at the supermarket without the whispers and glares was completely new to me. It was the first taste of freedom I knew in my adult life.

For a long time I had no choice but to remain in Wilton. If I didn't have Grandmother's house, I wouldn't have been able to take care of myself. Grandmother said she would never sell the house. She spent her entire life in Wilton, and she was going to die there. She didn't care that people talked. She didn't care what they said. As time went on I came and went. If I was able to manage on my own, I lived in Brockton, or Fall River, and eventually, north to Winter-hill. If things got bad and I was hospitalized, I found myself back at Grandmother's until I was able to get back on my feet.

Going back to Wilton after being away I noticed the changes more readily. The old storefronts are fast-food and market chains. Factory Row is lined with discount malls and condominiums. The farms around the edge of town have all been developed into suburbs. Now that Grandmother is gone and the house is sold, I can't imagine any reason to return to

Wilton ever again. When I went there to sign the last of the papers, I had to strain to see people I recognized as I drove through town. I saw one of the Donovan brothers with his wife and their kids coming out of a pizza shop. Mike Kelly, who sniffed glue with Harry and later bought pot from my mother, who went to jail for breaking and entering, was wandering down Main Street, bloated and gray. Caroline La Farge, the head cheerleader, still looked wholesome and fit, walking into a bank dressed in preppy clothes with her two perfect-looking children.

I drove through the old neighborhood, down Foster Street, past Grandmother's house, down to the dead end and the duplexes where Harry lived. Harry's blue house was brown. I turned around, took a left on to Fulton and a right on to Clark Street. The six-apartment tenement was no longer dark gray but an ugly purple. There were windows open in Mother's corner apartment. I could see children jumping around and playing. I heard a woman's voice shouting go outside if you're not going to play nice I'm in no fucking mood for your shit.

I'm cleaning a house which is made up of a

one-story series of long narrow connecting rooms. The building is windowless and I quickly lose track of the entrance. Room to room I clean asking various family members I encounter where the door is. Suddenly the mother of the house confronts me with an order to reclean one of the rooms. You could at least say please. We have words back and forth over who is in charge. The next thing I know I'm in one of the rooms and the family members are all lying around the floor with blood pouring out from gashes and I have a knife in my hand thinking that I will be blamed even though I know that I didn't do it. The mother comes out from nowhere and attacks me. In self-defense I stab her continually. I hear and feel the blade tearing into flesh until she falls dead.

I had my most intense sex with Nancy. I never liked cocaine. It has the opposite effect on me than it has on most people. I get more withdrawn and paranoid. But when Nancy put a little on my clitoris and did the things she did, it was something I'd never experienced. The problem was Nancy wanted to be my savior. I should be in college, I should do this or that. She bought me books, magazines, a portable television on my birthday because she couldn't stand the fact that I spent my free time sitting in the easy chair staring off into space. The harder she tried to change me, the more frustrated she became until she began to be mean. I didn't mind the intense sex, but sometimes I wanted to be softer and gentle but the rougher the better she said. I knew she went out on me. Everyone was after her. Men too. She was an Italian beauty with dark curly hair, green eyes, olive skin and the kind of body women kill for, with oversize breasts, a thin waist and long legs.

Aaron didn't mind what I did or didn't do, as long as I didn't bother him about staying out late and drinking. He was gentle and patient. I felt safe with him and trusted him. Aaron was fond of sailing and owned small boat which he docked at the harbor. Several occasions he packed a picnic lunch and we sailed around Boston harbor. I can see him sitting at the back steering with a can of beer in his hand, looking out in every direction with a content smile. Aaron didn't talk much and talked less out on the boat. Those were some of the most peaceful times I've ever known. We sailed, gazed at the skyline, and waved to other boaters passing by.

When we were hungry Aaron dropped anchor and we ate in silence in some out-of-the-way island cove. As the day wore on Aaron became drunk but he steadfastly kept control over the boat and got us back home as it was darkening.

No one would be interested in me now. It's not that I overeat any longer. In fact, I eat less than I ever did. I've never been able to lose much weight. I don't exercise. I see people out running in the streets or working out on treadmills and bike machines in the window of the fitness center. I see Harry doing a flying leap to make a game-winning catch. Everyone surrounds her, the boys lift her up on their shoulders and carry her off the field. Harry with her right arm up in her air, fist clenched.

Eight

Mother sometimes claimed they ran off one night and eloped. He lived with her off and on at the Clark Street apartment. Ray looked right through you as if you weren't there. He was dark and muscular with a thick head of black hair which he greased back. In the summer he went around shirtless and his arms and chest were tattooed. He wore a bushy mustache, chain smoked, his next cigarette always placed behind his right ear, and when he lit that one he replaced it with another from his pack. It was difficult to understand him because his manner of speech was a low mumble. On Monday nights Mother and Ray played cards with friends, drinking and smoking until early morning. Ray would get into fights over the games and once punched my mother's friend's boyfriend from across the table.

Ray's first wife divorced him before they had kids. He had two children with his second wife, who lived out of state. He owned a junkyard near Fall River and Mother met him on her waitress job. It wasn't until later we found out about his past. Mother was fond of borrowing his white Cadillac convertible and driving around Wilton. Grandmother put her out when Mother was beginning to see him. It wasn't because of Ray. Grandmother gave Mother several warnings, but Mother wouldn't stop selling pot out of Grandmother's house. There was no room for us at the Clark Street apartment, so Denise and I remained with Grandmother. At first, Ray was there all the time. Then they started fighting and police were frequently called by neighbors until eventually he was barred.

In less than five minutes I can clean my one room with its minuscule kitchenette and a tinier bathroom. I have one dresser half full of clothes and a small closet with room to spare. I own a pair of sneakers and construction boots. Food no longer carries the importance it once did for me, and I heat soup out of the can or make toast.

I failed when I first tried to move away from Grandmother's and make it on my own. But it was only until I moved far enough away from Wilton I was able to stay away. There had to be enough space so that it made it that much harder for me to go back. Roommates I vaguely remember, various apartments, jobs, hospitalizations. Sometimes Grandmother took the train to Boston to visit me in the hospital. When I was well enough I would take the train to visit her. However, I found that the longer I was away from Wilton, the more painful the infrequent visits on me. Grandmother said she understood and would understand if I found it impossible to return. She found it impossible to leave.

I started the cleaning business on my own. I placed notices up around neighborhoods and in the local papers. It took a while, but, eventually, I got a call. It was the Hales. They were my first clients. If I liked clothes, I could buy anything I wanted now. I could buy a new car. My old Datsun has been out in the street buried in a snow bank since the second big snow storm of the season. I take public transportation and walk the last stretch to the Hales'. Since they are my only clients, I leave all my cleaning equipment there. Mrs Hale always questions my bills, how much window cleaner or floor wax I use and how they're only responsible for what supplies I use in their house. I remind her that they are my only clients, everything I buy I use in her home, and she signs the check as if she's doing it under protest.

There was a time when I was reading much and I had designs on going to college and studying psychiatry. After receiving my high-school equivalency, I took some courses at the local community college. I was working days cleaning house, and going to school part-time evenings. That was after Aaron and before Nancy. One of the longest periods I've gone making progress. But then I got sick again and fell behind in school work. I tried to catch up later, but I couldn't and I never went back. Nancy brought home the forms so I could register again and went so far as fill them out for me. All you have to do is sign them. I wouldn't.

Harry paid school no attention. She made cheat sheets and slipped them up her sleeve or under her dress. Even in elementary school, where there was no way you could skip school without getting caught, Harry would skip. She took the train to Boston, or the bus to Fall River, and suffered the consequences. Standard punishment at home was a strapping at the hands of her father. Harry dropped her pants or lifted her skirt to display the strap welts on her thighs. It really isn't that bad and it's over in a few seconds.

Grandmother never put a hand on me or Denise, though there were times Denise warranted it with her swearing and being disrespectful to Grandmother. Mother broke a wooden spoon over my head when she was on the phone and trying to talk. I was in the kitchen fighting with Denise. It was the closest thing she could grab but it didn't hurt. Mother would throw things, or swing at you. But it never really hurt. She yelled and blew off steam then it was over.

Mother told me lies about my father. He did send money. She said he abandoned us both without any thought. Grandmother told me that one time my father sent a ticket to fly me to California and visit him. Mother sold the ticket. Grandmother kept much of this from me when I was young. She said she just wanted to protect me. At Christmas there were gifts, at least in the early years. A box of candy. Another time he sent a small wooden house with tiny carved people and furniture to put inside.

My dreams come right back upon wakening. Or later in the day one might surface from the depths and seize me. I'm never certain if I dreamed the dream the night before, or just remembered a version of it. On the seventy-seven bus, I'm suddenly walking with Harry. We've skipped school, though it is night. We are in a part of town we don't recognize, near the highway, the back side of one of the old factories. We come out from an alley, around a corner, and walk into a small lot that is a dead end. At the far end of the lot is a car full of men. We see them just as they see us. Harry says turn around and keep walking like everything's fine. There's the roar of an engine then tires squealing. They're coming right for us. Run Harry says run.

Because I take the same bus at the same time every day, I recognize people who regularly ride the seventy-seven. There's a smart-looking young couple too cool for anyone who giggle and whisper to each other; the guy who gets on at Warren Street is a little slow and has something wrong with his eyes, it's like they only open half-way; an elderly Portuguese man in some kind of green work uniform always studies any of the young girls aboard; and a large Haitian woman is already sitting at the very front of the bus when I get on.

I read the ads on the bus over and over. They change every two months. I can go to school evenings, learn one of a hundred languages, electronics or broadcasting. Am I tired and bored with my present job? I've never considered a career in the navy. There are so many ways to invest my money, how do I know my investor has my best interest in mind? How will I know? And I will not leave the Hales' until I have something to do. It's not that I need the money. It's what to do with my time.

The Hales live in one of the most expensive areas around. Those who live there call it the Quad, a quadrant of residential land that is wedged in the back side of Harvard Square in Cambridge. Big, beautiful old houses owned by beautiful old families adorn large tree- and lawn-lined streets. When my cleaning business was going at its height, I was cleaning six different homes in the Quad. I made a lot of money. I just put it in the bank. I did it because six of houses kept me busy six days a week ten hours a day. But it wasn't enough. I crashed. And came back. And crashed again. Now it's just the Hales. If Mr Hale wasn't a psychiatrist, and Mrs Hale so afraid of hiring a new cleaner, they would have let me go too.

Nine

Grandmother said although Grandfather was capable of being a mean man, inside he was a good man. In the beginning, he seemed like a nice Irish boy and her family liked him; but as the years went on, his family's problems became more apparent, as did my grandfather's. It wasn't easy for him growing up she said. She could be forgiving like that. If she didn't have much good to say about a person, Grandmother said little. If I knew the family Grandfather came from she told me, I would understand his actions better.

When Mother moved out her reason for getting a small apartment was money. She said when she had more, she'd get a bigger place and we could go with her. At least the Clark Street apartment was close by and she could be near her girls. Mornings on the way to school I'd see

Ray's convertible parked out front. One night Harry and I were coming back from the movies and the police were in front of Mother's place because she and Ray had a fight. Ray was enraged, swearing out in the middle of the street while the police were trying to control him. Another officer was sitting with my mother on the apartment steps, she had her face in her hands, crying. Ray kept calling her a fucking slut. There were many people gathered around the scene who knew me and my family. The cops made Ray drive away and helped Mother back into the apartment. Then people were beginning to stare at me and I hurried off embarrassed.

Under my arms the smell changes over the course of days. Same with my scalp, vagina and my feet. From the clean-soap smell after a shower to the first hints of sweat and fluids. After several days the various bodily odors take on fouler essences. The direct rankness of my armpits. The earthy potato smell of my ear wax. The fishy urine smell of my vagina. The sweaty sneaker-sock smell of my feet. The secretious muddy smell of my scalp. All of them at the tips of my fingers.

During a treatment they put a breathing bag over my mouth. Someone stands next to me throughout the procedure, squeezing air into my lungs so that I don't stop breathing. I'm a blank sheet of paper when I leave the hospital. What is clear are the simple, concrete things. I walk. I see. I sip tea. I smoke a cigarette. The day is gray or blue. I sleep an hour or two. I keep everything away, or I think I do because in actuality I have no control. A light, a shadow, a voice. Enough time passes, probes into my memory. A fleeting look into a dream. A song on a passing car radio. Brings something back.

We were her angels, darlings, sweet things. But never her children. Never I love you. She seemed to be broke every time Christmas or a birthday came around so Grandmother bought gifts and planned parties that Mother failed to attend. Denise wanted the big birthday parties with two dozen kids and presents and all the attention on her. I hated parties. I only wanted my favorite orange spice cake which Grandmother made for me. When I fought with Denise she used situations like this to be hurtful. You don't even have any friends to invite to a party.

Denise leaves two messages in a day. Then one the following day. I return her call. How am I she was worried sick when I didn't call right back. Take a trip out to visit in California. Dan wants to meet her family, he'll pay for my first-class ticket round trip. I'll love it out there. Wait until I see her house and the pool and take a drive in Dan's refinished Corvette. I can come now, or later when the baby comes. She'll probably need some help then. Can I believe the way it's worked out for her after all these years.

Every time something new comes along, usually a man, it's the right one and this is what she's been waiting for all her life. Now is not a good time. There's much I have to take care of here. Maybe later after the baby comes. I say these words to Denise but I don't believe them. I don't want to see her. I don't want to see her baby when it is born. I don't want to go to California, except to find my father's grave. Denise will suck me in and suck me dry.

There have been at least two abortions with her past men. Dan's the oldest of all her men at sixty. But I'm glad she has Dan. If she were without a man right now, I wouldn't have one peaceful moment until she had what she saw as her rightful share to Grandmother's money. She plays people like marbles Harry said. I know she's your sister, but don't trust her. Harry could talk with a kid for a few minutes and come away with an astute assessment. That kid's got a lot of problems. That girl thinks every boy is in love with her.

Harry said she knew about her brother Eddie. What was the big deal? I tried it again with Harry, after I went all the way with Billy Donovan and Brian Walsh who I went steady with for two weeks. It didn't seem right. It wasn't like the time years before on Bear Hill. I just kept thinking that this was my friend Harry I was kissing. I let Harry have her way a little with me and helped her to an orgasm. But after that I avoided that kind of stuff with her and we started to see less of each other.

I learned that my mother was pregnant with Jennifer from Harry. I told Grandmother who turned bright red, then completely pale. Mother said she intended to surprise us with the news. We assumed that Ray was the father. It hurt me that Harry knew more about my mother's personal life than me. I didn't see Mother much then. Once a week maybe, except for a wave hello if she drove by and I was out around the neighborhood. Harry was at the Clark Street apartment a lot, buying pot, hanging around when the weather was cold. Now whenever I saw Harry she was high or wanted to get high.

It wasn't as if I was losing my mother. She was never mine to lose. Harry was my savior. Outside of my grandmother she was all I had and she got me through. Now, even when I saw her, she was growing distant and withdrawn as she smoked more. Somewhere around that time Harry's brother Eddie was arrested for breaking into houses. Eddie hung around Dad's Variety. Dad was a heavy old man who chewed stubby cigars. In addition to cigarettes, milk and bread, Dad sold small appliances like radios and toasters. Harry said that the merchandise was stolen. I don't know what else Dad did, but Eddie was one of a regular group of older boys, most of them who quit school and used Dad's as a kind of home away from home.

Eddie had to go to the reform school in Plymouth for three months because it was the second time he was arrested. I don't know why, but when Eddie was at Plymouth, Harry ran away again. I wasn't even aware she was on the run until I called on her one day and her folks acted uneasy and said Kathleen wasn't there and started asking me when was the last time I'd seen her. Billy Donovan told me Harry was hiding out in the woods at Bear Hill Reservation during the day, and at night she was sneaking into town and staying at my mother's apartment on Clark Street. I ran over to my mother's apartment. There were two people there who Mother said worked with her at the bar. They didn't stay long and after they left I confronted my mother about Harry. It wasn't true and she didn't know where I got my information from but she hadn't seen Harry in days.

I hurried home to fetch my bike. I peddled furiously towards Bear Hill Reservation. There were miles of woods and Harry could be anywhere but I didn't care. Fate, I assumed, would direct me to her. I negotiated the rotary around Route 133 and started in on one of the woods roads. My body had worked up a sweat from my ride, and now that I was in the woods it was cooler and there was a breeze that said autumn was around the corner. The forest was still in late-summer green, but tinges of red and yellow could be detected on leaf tips. There were people walking dogs and a bunch of stoned laughing boys. I asked all of them if they'd seen a girl about my age with blond hair. None of them had, though one of the stoned boys said he wished he had and the others all broke up laughing.

I knew Harry's spots in the woods, places she'd taken me to over the years. I buried my bike in some brambles and went ahead on foot to Gone Place which was right behind Meadow Pond. Gone Place was so close to the pond where everyone picnicked and swam during the summertime you could hear all the shrieks and life-guard whistles, but you were completely alone and sealed off from the crowd. Harry first showed me the footpath, it was only a short walk up through thick underbrush to a small clearing. Under pine trees and years and years of fallen pine needles lay the softest natural bed. She wasn't there.

She wasn't at Indian Ground either, the place where kids went to party. The spot was marked by large, dead and burned-out trees which lent the area a strange and forbidding air. It was nestled on the back side of Little Bear Hill and you could see miles of woods spreading out towards Brockton. Indian Ground, Harry said, was sacred and kids should be respectful when they party there. My last chance was My Ground. Harry said nobody knew about it except her, until she took me there. There were no trails. It was just a spot. Nothing special about it. You'd walk right past it without a notice. Harry knew exactly where the spot of My Ground was. She said she came upon it by accident one day, but as soon as she found herself there, she had a peculiar feeling and knew it would be her own sacred place. She never approached the place the same way twice; so she never wore a foot path there. I only knew it was between Corser Brook and what we called the Old Mine Road although there was never any evidence of an old mine. I started walking a criss-cross pattern between the brook and the road. I knew she had to be at My Ground. It was the only spot where Harry could go when she absolutely wanted to be alone. I called out her name. I called out her name again. Harry, it's me Laurel.

Ten

One day the temperature is in single digits. The next day it's fifty degrees. Yesterday was blizzard-like snows. Today is spring rain. Water drips off four sides of the house, tapping ceaselessly in irregular rhythms.

There was a windy day in March, after a long cold spell, suddenly one day was seventy-five degrees and Dilboy Park overflowing with kids. Dad's Variety sold out of ten-cent kite kits, by mid-afternoon most of them lay in hundreds of pieces on the park floor. Harry's brother Eddie bought a one-dollar kite at a hobby shop in Brockton and he and Harry flew that kite so high we could barely see it. Harry and Eddie stood ground below, taking turns holding the wooden handle with the kite string wrapped around it, eyes to the heavens, serious in their communication with each other – let a little out, take a little in – intent on keeping that kite up there as high and for as long as they were able.

I don't know what I would do without cigarettes. The medications come three times a day. It's not like I notice them in a way that I feel high, but everything's held at a distance so that I'm able to move safely, if only inside my head. The joy of cigarettes is endless with each deep breath, smoke and fire, hand to mouth.

Grandmother didn't drive so after Grandfather died she sold his car. Once or twice during each summer, however, she took us by bus to Singing Sands Beach near Plymouth. She packed sandwiches, cookies, fruit and soda into a big basket and Denise and I took along whatever beach toys we could find. As we grew older, I enjoyed these ocean-side excursions less and less; I was becoming more self-conscious about my body and embarrassed by my exaggerated roundness. I sat on the blanket wearing cut-offs, a t-shirt and big hat while Denise pranced around in her bikini entertaining all the males in the immediate vicinity. A few times Harry came along. She always wore a one-piece suit, even though she had a better figure than Denise. The boys checked out Harry too, but Harry didn't care and she never flaunted it. I never liked the smell of the ocean. High tide was bearable and had a certain crispness, but low tide turned my stomach sour.

Some green teas are low in caffeine, others higher. Some are laced with various herbs. I used milk and sugar. Then honey. And now just black. It doesn't matter how high or low in caffeine my sleep is never affected. The part of a cup I like least is when I get near the bottom and it's had time to cool, the bottom-of-the-cup sediments turn bitter. I drink it, sediment and all, listening to my stomach gurgle deep and long.

My late twenties I call my suicide period. I never directly attempted to take my own life, though many times I seriously contemplated it. I was drinking very heavily, taking the drugs my doctors prescribed as well as cocaine and pills that I could buy. Grandmother was horrified but helpless to do anything. In one of my stays in the hospital I met a guy who was getting ECT for his crazy behavior. When I was released he asked me if he could call me when he got better and I never thought when I gave him my number he actually would. Vanity can come out of nowhere and suddenly I was derailed. He was a small and thin guy, but handsome. The idea that someone so attractive could be interested in me was enough.

I began to hang around with his friends. They were mostly my age, a few were from Wilton but many were from the outlying small towns and places like New Bedford. They were druggies who always had a little money but never seemed to work. I had a crazy affair with Teddy. It was a party day and night. Then we broke up and I started sleeping with a friend of his. I wouldn't go home at night. I woke up drank and drugged myself into obliteration until I woke again. I slept with anyone who had a bed. It was mostly with guys, though several of the women in the group were topless dancers who were more interested in other women off hours. For a brief period I became involved with one named Sunny, but she had more problems than I did and we were doomed from the start. Once I woke up in a bathtub full of ice water because I passed out from drinking too much Jack Daniel's and taking too many pills. Another time I had to be rushed to the hospital and had my stomach pumped. It didn't last

long, that period of my life. A year, two at the
most. Then I was back in the hospital for
treatments and when Grandmother got me
home she managed to keep those people away.

If I fly to California to see Denise I can visit
my father's grave. They are in completely
different parts of the state. I don't want to see
her; and I don't know for sure if I want to see
his grave. Hold on tight he said when I rode him
like a horse and he pranced around the living
room of our old house on all fours making
horse sounds. Another game of ours was I'll get
you, where he chased me around saying I'll get
you I'll get you. I ran excitedly ahead, and he
allowed me to remain just out of reach until I
finally ran out of breath and he caught me,
raised me up over his shoulders, and played me
like a trombone as he marched around the living
room.

Except for Harry, my closest friends in school
were two teachers. Mrs Macken was my home
economics teacher, and Miss Wilkins my
seventh-grade English teacher. Miss Wilkins
was from the South and spoke with an accent.
She was pretty, and youthful. She was born
with some kind of birth defect and had no

fingers on her left hand. When we had to write stories or reports, she often read mine aloud to the class as an example. Sometimes after school I wandered into her room and sat in the front row while she readied to leave and we chatted about how she ended up in Wilton coming from Virginia and what was college like in Boston. I told her about my home life, she said my grandmother sounded like a fine woman. Then one day she announced that she was leaving to get married. The following Monday morning she was gone. Mrs Hill, a mean, tired-of-teaching older woman who banged the top of her desk with her fist and yelled damn damn damn this class, took over. I never saw Miss Wilkins after that.

The warm spell melts all the snow. My car has been left with a locked boot on the wheel and was sideswiped while it was buried under the snow during the winter. At the traffic office I pay the money to have the boot removed. The car won't start and needs repairs. It's fifteen years old and I don't have the energy to deal with it. I dial a number in the phone book. The ad that says highest money paid for your junk car turns out to be a guy saying it will cost me fifty dollars to have him come and take it away. I don't really need a car. I only had one because when the cleaning business was going I had to have means to get my equipment and supplies around. I pay the man the fifty and watch him tow the car away. It is cold and getting colder. This week will be a blue moon.

I don't know where I will be three or four or six months from now. There are so many people in this city it is easy just to wash out. No one notices anything. I've had several treatments while living in this space, and the people directly above me haven't a clue. I tell them I've been visiting a relative or away on vacation. Since most of them don't understand English it's not difficult.

In my life there are two places where I have felt grounded. The first house, with my father and mother, though I was so young I vaguely remember any concrete details, and those that I do recall might be only in my imagination. The second place is Grandmother's house, although later it became like a slow torture chamber, despite her support and love. I couldn't get out of the loop there. A light. A shadow. A voice. When the weather improves I'll purchase one of those train passes and go around the country stopping at different cities. I'll see places I've never seen and experience different landscapes and people. Perhaps in some far off city, town, or state I could never have imagined, I'll find a place where I want to stay.

Eleven

I see my therapist every other week now. She is an American-raised Japanese woman, petit, attractive, shiny black hair, skin like porcelain, brilliant mind. I fantasize about her.

As I get older doctors and therapists look younger. She is younger than me by ten years. My experiences with therapists have been anything from total failures to an occasional breakthrough. There was a brutish old man who took an impatient attitude with me and somehow implied that my problems were all brought on by me. There was a woman who sat and stared. She never said a word during my entire session. She sat and stared at me, visit after visit. Dr Isu is the best yet, though I guess she's only been out of school a few years. She can listen, respond, and be supportive. She knows everything there is to know about me. It's as if she's a best friend except I pay her.

She was the one who suggested we meet every other week. I was afraid that the longer I am away, the easier it is to slide into my old thought patterns; the easier it is to think I don't need a therapist and see my therapist as part of my problem; the easier it is to play with the doses of my medication, come apart and wind up in treatment again. If you don't do something about it yourself, you'll continue the same pattern for the rest of your life the old brute therapist barked at me.

I'm walking through the park, it's late at night and the light at the basketball court is shut off. I'm half-way across the park, directly in the center, where no light from street lights is able to reach. Harry appears from shadows and startles me. She says that everything's all right. She smiles and begins one of her silly free-form dances. Where have you been Harry? Stop it Harry. Tell me where you have been.

When I do the Hales' hardwood floors with oil soap it takes me the exact number of mop strokes every week. I clean the same four-foot square sections at a time. In one hour I can do the wooden floors on all levels. The new cook is already complaining to me how the Hales only want to pay him from the time he shows up at the house, while, at the same time, they expect him to stop at the grocery store on his drive in. I've heard it all before. He's a strange, large man perhaps my age. He has a look in his eye, the look I've seen before, like he's seeing something else in addition to what's in his field of vision. He talks to himself in the kitchen. I'll punch you in the fucking face. Listen motherfucker I'll rip your heart out. He was a musician and his cousin was someone famous who I never heard of. Person to person, he has a sweet, gentle demeanor. The Hales love his cooking and he likes the kids.

Once my mother had a dog. It was a birthday gift from a boyfriend, a fluffy white thing about the size of a cat. Her name was Ginger. She peed and shat all over Grandmother's house and since mother was never around Grandmother and I cleaned up and made sure the dog got fed, watered and walked. No matter how many times I walked her, Ginger preferred to relieve herself in the house. When Mother was around, she paid more attention to Ginger than she did to me or Denise. She would fuss over her, pet her, kiss her, talk to her like a little child. Then one day Ginger got out of the house. Harry and I went all over the place on our bikes looking for her. The next morning a police car pulled up, the officers had Ginger's collar. She was hit by a car and killed on Main Street. I ran to my room and cried hard. I felt like it was my fault she was loose in the first place. Grandmother said it was no one's fault, we couldn't watch Ginger twenty-four hours a day. Mother cried hysterically, trying to blame us for not watching the dog closer. Grandmother told her it wasn't our dog and Mother was lucky we did what we had done for Ginger.

I never liked pets after that. Cats I especially don't trust. And I can't stand the smell of those odor boxes. Denise's second husband owned a horse farm on the Wilton-Townsend line. She had an expensive black horse while she was married and spent a small fortune on equipment, clothes and private riding lessons. Then she had a fall and broke her wrist and never rode again. She and her husband lived in a big farmhouse that was remodeled. There was a pool and many acres of land. Everything was going so well and the next thing she cut her wrists again. He was a monster she couldn't live with. There were stories about physical and mental abuse. Even though she's my sister, I'm never sure what to believe. Since I can remember, Denise has never been able to distinguish between truth and lies.

The woman upstairs does chores any hour of the day or night. Hers are the heaviest footsteps. They are all overweight, but she is the heaviest, square jaw, square shoulders, square frame, black square-cut dress, dark square-cut hair. I hear her footsteps back and forth in the kitchen, up and down the cellar stairs where she has a load of laundry going. I hear her footsteps ascend the creaky stairs between the two floors of her apartment. She blows her nose loud and long. I cannot let go of a vivid memory I have of her, the first summer I lived here. One afternoon I walked down the driveway, I paused looking for the keys to my basement door. I heard the back door close and she came down the stairs in all her abundant squareness, holding a large round platter overflowing with raw red meat she intended to grill. In one hand she had a long two-pronged fork, in the other she carried the platter, full of rings of orange sausage, bloody steaks and fleshy pink chops. There was enough meat to feed a dozen people but there are only three adults. They always cook like that. She smiled a wide gold-capped smile and said the only word she knows in English, a long drawn out hiiiii.

Mother was miserable when she was pregnant with baby Jennifer. She was fighting a lot with Ray. Then they were going to be married. Ray was the love of her life. And he was going to be the father of her baby. She continued to smoke and drink and work nights at the lounge, and she was impossible to be around. Her outbursts, which she could always take to extreme limits, became more frequent and irrational. Grandmother was worried that she might lose the baby, and urged her to move back into the house with us. Mother insisted that once she and Ray were married, they were going to buy a big house outside of town, then she could take us and Grandmother wouldn't have to be put out one more day. Mother could be cruel to Grandmother and say things like I know you don't want me or my kids here.

For several weeks Mother planned a wedding and spent her free hours making arrangements.

She scheduled a justice of the peace, planned a party at a local hall and hired a band. The next thing the wedding was off and they broke up again. Harry alluded to the fact that Ray was never sure if the baby was his. Harry also told me that on several occasions Ray had hit my mother. It was nothing that I ever noticed in terms of bruises, but he slapped her face and pushed her around when things got heated between them. Harry said that she didn't like Ray, there was something about him she couldn't trust but my mother was blinded by love. I don't think my mother ever knew what love was; Ray was the most available guy with the most money.

Until I was in therapy, I always thought Grandmother was perfect. She was my savior. But in trying to be perfect, one makes mistakes. Sometimes I feel that Denise might have turned out better if Grandmother gave her the same kind of attention that she gave me. And Grandmother always said that I was the good one, and she didn't know what happened with Denise. In a way she was right. But Denise always said that Grandmother loved me and not her and Mother didn't love either of us. Looking back

Grandmother made it very clear that she favored me.

In therapy, I started to see things differently. You get shaken up that way and all the usual defense mechanisms get eaten away. You think yourself innocent and realize no one is. You think someone perfect and realize you only want them to be perfect so you see them accordingly. You think you acted one way for one reason, only to find the opposite to be true.

Twelve

There are two dozen various cleaners in the box where I store my supplies. Glass cleaners, floor cleaners, floor waxes, hardwood-floor oils, disinfectants, bowl and tile cleaners, grease cutters, stove cleaners, laundry detergents, bleaches. By the time I am finished with my work, the Hales' house reeks of the disparate chemicals. It's a seductive bouquet, and I find myself breathing deep and slow through my nostrils. I smell Grandmother's house. I see her glistening kitchen floor and the waxy sheen of the red pine floorboards in the humble living room; the glistening tiled bathroom; clean folded stacks of laundry I could bury my face in and smell fresh air.

Nancy ate a strict vegetarian diet. Drugs were fine but meat wasn't. She wouldn't take any dairy, to my dismay, since, at the time, ice cream was big in my diet. It's all chemicals she said. Our bodies are made up of nothing but chemicals, like the universe. She was like that. She frequently waxed philosophical. She usually quoted from something she'd recently read in one of the books she was always trying to get me to read. You need to overcome your dominant paradigm she said after reading one.

Sometimes when I am finished cleaning at the Hales', I open the windows to let in fresh air. Grandmother called it airing out the house. In the middle of winter, several times a week after her house-cleaning was finished, she opened every window in the house, regardless of the temperature, to let the bad air out and the good air in. A practice I continue with my cleaning, though Mrs Hale disapproves of wasting heat in winter or the central air conditioning in summer. Grandmother had no spray bottles and miracle cleaners. She mixed her one cleaner with water, varying the cleaner-to-water ratio with each job. She scrubbed standing, she scrubbed on her hands and knees, toting around with rubber-gloved hands her blue bucket filled with soapy warm water.

Mother's Clark Street apartment was filthy.

She hated natural light and the shades were drawn day or night. It was because of how she looked. You see all the lines in daylight she said. As beautiful as she still was, in those days she lived on Clark Street, in the morning her face lines and shaky hands showed a woman five or ten years older. It got so bad there, a fetid smell overwhelmed you when you walked through the door, a combination of stale beer, cigarette and pot smoke, dust and beefy grease. Ray was fond of frying hamburgers and the dishes and pans stacked up in the sink. There was no way Grandmother wanted Mother to take baby Jennifer, but Grandmother had no choice. She couldn't turn her only daughter in. And Clark Street was close enough so we had Jennifer most of the time anyway. Mother was trying to get back at Ray, somehow she thought having the baby living with her would help.

Every day Grandmother or I went to Mother's to bring Jennifer back. Many nights Jennifer slept over with us. Other nights Mother hired a baby-sitter, one of her co-workers' teenage daughters, or one of the girls to whom she sold pot. Grandmother and I never trusted any of them and dropped in unexpectedly so the sitters knew we were close by and keeping an eye out. One time Caroline Mason was watching Jennifer and when we dropped in she was in the middle of having a party. There were a dozen kids there, all of them I knew from the neighborhood or school. They were drinking beer, smoking pot and cigarettes, and Grandmother threw them all out. We took Jennifer home with us and the next morning Mother showed up at the house screaming at Grandmother she had no right to do what she did. Grandmother threatened she could report her to the social services department.

Everybody knew my business, and in some cases, more of it than I did. After the night when Grandmother and I found Caroline Mason partying with the kids, I couldn't look at any of them in the eye and felt ashamed, as if it was my fault. I was estranged from part of my family and the kids in the neighborhood. Denise had no problem. She acted as if nothing out of ordinary was going on. If she was mad at Mother, Mother was the enemy and she went on campaigns to undermine her. When she was getting along well with Mother, she used her whenever she could for things like money or a ride somewhere.

It's easy for me to lose track of the day of the week or time of the day. I'm only at the Hales' three or four hours a day, three days a week, and the rest of the time I'm here. I am never completely alone. There are sounds coming from upstairs or outside. I am never completely in the dark because, day or night, some semblance of light slips in from somewhere. Days and nights are a continuum. I lay on the bed. I sip green tea. I smoke. My short stints of sleep may come any time and the moments of waking are most confusing as it may take as much as a minute for me to retrace my steps back to where I am at the moment.

They keep the television on very loud upstairs. Often it's tuned to the Portuguese station. At night the little girl watches the same American shows I hear the Hale kids talking about. The grandfather listens to soccer games on the radio, the rise and fall of the announcer's voice and roar of the crowds fill my room, especially in the summer when he sits in the yard at the picnic table, sipping his red wine with the transistor radio next to him. Mother always had the television or the radio turned on loud. She never turned it down when I asked, so I often had to lay awake at night waiting for her to fall asleep so I could get up and turn it off. She'd come home from a shift late at night and watch reruns of old black and white movies. If she wasn't completely asleep when I entered her room to shut off the television, she'd bark out leave it alone I'm still watching it.

I have no television or radio. I don't read the newspapers or magazines. But there's no way to cut myself off from any of it. On buses, in markets, at the Hales', people talk about what's on television and what's in the news. The most recent murder. The big game. The terrible parents who were shooting their children with drugs and having sex with them. There's no way to avoid it. Someone on the bus has a newspaper or magazine open and my eye is drawn to a headline. The Hales have a television running on every floor sometimes. Television journalists prying their way into the face of some grieving woman whose child has just been found raped and strangled. There's a country some-where that we are bombing. People are starving. Prep School Prof. Kept Kiddie Porn.

Having spent so much time in institutions, I've learned to recognize certain characteristics in people. Denise, for example, is like other women I've met, who cut themselves like some people get hair cuts. They act out. They stalk. They cling. They claw. It started with her at an early age and really escalated once she hit puberty. Fact and fiction are one. When she told me about what happened with Ray I didn't believe it, at first. Then I thought back to those times. She was twelve or thirteen. The backyard cookouts at Grandmother's. Ray with his shirt off and Denise with her short shorts and tight tops sitting on his knee. They never went all the way. She said they mostly made out when they had a minute or two alone. Ray would feel her up some, but that's as far as it went. When mother was pregnant and crazy to be around, she said she and Ray got into it more often, right up through the time that baby Jennifer was born. The one who forced her against her will was Al. I hardly remember Al, he was before Ray and it only lasted a month or two.

One night Denise took her bike to the lounge where my mother worked to bring Mother something she'd forgotten, most probably pot.

This guy Al was hanging out at the bar and offered to put Denise's bike in the back of his pickup truck and drive her home. Mother thought it a great idea. On the way home the guy pulled off Route 133 into the woods where he raped her. Denise said he told her if she ever breathed a word about it to anyone, he would claim she was a liar and that everyone already knew her reputation and they would believe him. I didn't know these things at the time. I learned them from Denise in bits and pieces. But sometimes her stories changed.

With someone like Dr Isu, I might consider having a relationship with a woman again. She wears no ring. But that doesn't mean anything. Her mannerisms don't offer the slightest clue as to her sexual preference. It's not her looks, which I do find attractive, but something that comes from deep inside her. She's gentle, wise, sensitive; and has no mean spirit. At least none that I can detect. But I only see her forty-five minutes at a time the same time every other week. And it's her job to be gentle, wise and sensitive. Who knows what she's like on a bad day wearing her darkest suit.

Dr Hale has all of these traits. In public, he is

celebrated for his humanistic achievements, loved and respected by his peers and the public. But he is not the same person at home where he is controlling. This is easily disguised as an overcaring virtue in public; but in private it is potent and stings. On the surface is the jolly we're-all-in-this-together family personality; but, in a passive way, things go his way or no way. The piano lessons. The voice lessons. The sports the kids choose. The vacations or family days out. How Mrs Hale wears her hair. Everything is centered around what he wants, needs and thinks is best.

So some people have different personalities, depending on the situation. I have been the same person for too long. As much as I sometimes think otherwise, a relationship is not going to change that. I've learned that already. It's not that I prefer women. I would love the love of a man. But most of them are so simplistic. No one would want me. I'd have to lose weight. Fix my hair. Go out. I can't imagine having someone lying next to me here, interrupting my space, seeing my naked body. I would have to bath every day. They would have to know everything. They would want to know everything. They would want to put their hands on my flabby body and smell my smells and I would have to believe.

Thirteen

I try to imagine Grandmother's life and what it was like for her those last years alone in the house. The frequency of my visits coincided with my stability; but even when I was able, I visited less frequently in time. She grew frail as the years chipped away, although her mind remained sharp and clear.

On my visits she reported how she spent her days cleaning and preparing meals for herself. She had some spinach left over and broiled up a small steak. She washed the stairs going down to the basement, a task that was long overdue. Yesterday she made a nice chicken soup and she'll eat it through the week. She liked to preface her food descriptions with the word nice. On her soap opera a long lost twin brother of one of the main characters appeared out of nowhere, impersonating his brother. And the man came out the other day to look at the roof. It only needed to be patched in a few spots. She rarely went out, even her groceries were delivered.

Eventually she stopped lobbying for me to move back with her. She wanted me there, but she knew that I had to make a life somewhere beyond Wilton. I'm glad she didn't suffer and went in her sleep, although she was dead in her bed all those days. Her heart was the last thing I suspected would give out. She previously requested a funeral service in the church, and I buried her alongside Grandfather. I was the only family member at the service. The only other attendees were several old widows in black who attend mass daily, they sat in the back clutching their rosary beads. Until the week of her death, Grandmother attended church every Sunday morning. But she made no friends or contacts. God's enough to get me through the day. I sat in the front row of Grandmother's funeral, the priest's words echoing empty through the church, empty in my ears; I desperately wished what Grandmother believed in were true. In that event she might have peace in another world.

Harry can't hold herself up and falls off the Bear Hill tower. That's when I wake up. What really happened was she terrorized me for several seconds. We were hanging out at the tower, smoking cigarettes and hoping the boys we'd seen on our way up would follow. They did, and judging by the way they coughed when Harry lit them up, they never smoked before. We usually avoided going inside the tower because of the strong urine smell. It was built of fieldstone three stories high. That day we decided to walk up the spiral stairs to the lookout platform and see if the boys were coming. You could see the ocean way off in the distance on one side, and the forest stretching out to Brockton on the other.

Harry whispered in my ear they're virgins. On the top deck the conversation was awkward. Harry asked them if either of them had ever kissed a girl before. They both said sure. Harry said I don't believe you prove it. The boys got nervous and looked at each other and down at their shoes. Just at that instant, without any warning, Harry climbed over the railing and held herself up by her hands on the stone ledge. The drop was enough to seriously injure, if not kill her, and the two boys and I gasped. Harry was always capable of daredevil antics, but this was the most dangerous thing I'd ever seen her do. I screamed at her Harry what the fuck are you doing? The boys looked at each other and ran down the stairs in a panic. By the time I made any gesture to help, Harry was already pulling herself up over the ledge and back in again grinning the entire time. She jumped down on to the platform and brushed herself off. Scared the shit out of them she said as we watched those boys run down the trail and out of our sight. My heart was pounding. I grabbed her hard don't ever do that again.

When I was a child, Grandmother's house seemed big. But after I finally moved out and continued to visit her, the house grew wearily small. I didn't want to have to go back in there; but someone had to get Grandmother's things out of the house. Most of her possessions were old and there was nothing of value. The furniture. The curtains. The dishes, glasses, pots and pans. Every single object in that place oozed with some kind of flash memory. It was too much, and I had all I could do to have someone come in and haul it all away. A lifetime of her accumulations, cellar to attic, gone in a matter of a few hours.

I was forced to spend considerable time in Wilton after Grandmother died. First I had to make her funeral arrangements. Then the house needed to be cleared out and sold. It was over a decade since I left. The neighborhood changed. Houses were occupied by new families. It was possible to drive through Wilton to Grandmother's and not see anyone I recognized. Though at any particular time the sight of a certain street corner, fire escape, park bench, strip of fence, stretch of road, kids playing baseball or riding bikes, group of teenagers hanging out, or that lone girl bringing a cigarette to her lips like she owns the world, I saw Harry.

There were some personal items of Grandmother's and I knew where they were, including a few pieces of jewelry, a box with photos dating back from her wedding and following up through my mother's first wedding and various family gatherings on holidays, birthdays, my first holy communion. The newspaper clippings. I put everything in one big chest which sits at the foot of my bed. I don't want what's inside; I don't care to look inside. I owe it to her to keep these things. Her house didn't sell for as much as she would have thought. One is hard pressed to find a reason to be attracted to Wilton these days. And clean as it was on the inside, all those years of structural neglect left the house in need of serious repairs. I experienced a tremendous sense of relief the day I finally had no reason ever to return to Wilton.

Radio stations, television stations, newspapers. The headlines, photographs and film-clips. Triple-murder-suicide, black-and-white photos of victims, uniformed men carrying a body bag on a stretcher down a flight of stairs. Her chest sits at the foot of the bed. I must make a clean break. I can't move. My body is wrapped in gauze. A light. A shadow. A voice. Do you understand me? You are Laurel Bell. You have had a treatment. You are in . . .

Upstairs they fight. The little girl's mother and grandmother work during the day. The grandfather works through the night and sleeps through the morning and afternoon. This is fine when the little girl is at school, but during the summer when she is home there's always a ruckus going on because she's not allowed outside of the yard. I never see her with friends, and when I leave my apartment and she's out in the yard playing alone, she follows me to the end of the driveway asking where I am going when I'll be back. She says they never let me go anywhere. I can't leave the yard. When she gets bored in the yard she goes in the house and disrupts the grandfather's sleep and he yells and sometimes hits her. Recently she had a black eye and said she fell.

I fear the unknown as much as I fear what I know. Stillness. Quiet. Dark. Green tea and cigarettes. The heater clicks on. Dust rises and settles. Upstairs dishes are placed on the table. Lunch. Dinner. Breakfast. The grandmother shouts. They eat fast and voraciously, breaking bread with their hands in large chunks. I've seen them in the yard under the grape arbor. Germs gather in the minutest crevices. Smell of fatty sausage grease, cigarette smoke, my scalp. Sound of raised voices in a language foreign to me, conspiring to undermine the trajectory of my memory.

Denise says once I come out to California I won't want to return to Massachusetts. And there's absolutely no reason to with Grandmother gone. Mrs Hale's been trying to be closer and more sociable since she knows I no longer need the work. I don't understand how Denise will be able to parent. It's not as much selfishness but nature. It's the only way she can be. She won't accept the competition.

I wonder which ones they are. I am walking down the street, sitting on the bus, shopping at the market. How do they get on? What kind of marriages? What kind of parents? What kind of work? What kind of sleep? What kind of dreams? They are out there as close as the next seat.

I have met many over the years. Names and faces I forget. I remember the stories. The girl who watched her father murder her mother when she was five. The two sisters who were continually raped by their step-father for years while their mother knew. The girl who used to set fires. Even in the hospital she set fires, no matter how closely they watched her she managed to smuggle matches and get a fire going somewhere. Once she jammed her door shut and lit her bed and curtains on fire and they had to break down the door. The girl who counted her cuts which numbered in the hundreds. I've never once ran into one on the outside. At least anyone that I recognized. But we all go back out. We all have to go somewhere when they tell us we are ready.

Fourteen

Harry first showed me how to shoot a can of beer behind the Curtis School. First you puncture a hole in the lower side of the can, then flip the ring-top, hold the can upright and the beer shoots out the lower hole. Harry sucked the contents of a can down in seconds. When I tried, beer went all over my face and I gagged. I had to sneak into the house so Grandmother didn't catch me with the smell of beer. Harry loved beer, when she was drunk, she got even funnier, performing one-person shows or saying the most inappropriate things. She started to drink a lot, and as she got drunker, she became less able to carry on a coherent conversation and her physical agility gave way to a stumbling, falling kid who would pass out in the bushes behind the school. Unable to wake her, I left her to sleep it off.

She didn't tell me she was on the run that last time. I found out from Billy Donovan, who also informed me that Harry was living at my mother's apartment. I saw her there frequently when I picked up baby Jennifer or dropped her off; I thought nothing of it at the time. Ray wasn't living in the apartment because there were ugly fights and the police took Ray away in handcuffs and warned him to stay away. If Mother didn't need baby Jennifer as a pawn in her war with Ray, she would have let Jennifer just stay with us all the time.

Sister Agnes opens her arms with her palms flat-out towards the class, she tilts her head back, rolls her eyeballs up into the back of their sockets and says they nailed him to the cross. For several long seconds she stands there with her arms outstretched and her eyes rolled back. Then she speaks again. Imagine the spikes straight through his hands and feet, shaking her palms when she says the words spikes straight through his hands. And he hung there, blood oozing out of his wounds. Imagine what it must feel like to have spikes hammered through your hands and feet and to hang by those spikes. He suffered and he died for you. And she looks through us with piercing gray eyes, flat face, oversized lips, pasty skin. Then she looks up at the large carved crucifix hanging above the blackboard with glossy globs of red paint around the hand and foot wounds. And he hung there for you.

Harry could do a great imitation of Sister Agnes. Over the years, the phrase he hung there for you became a catch-all funny line which we used on each other, and as an in joke on others. Sometimes, out of nowhere, Harry would walk up to one of the neighborhood kids or a complete stranger on the street and say he hung there for you. And it always cracked me up. What I remember most about summer-vacation school, besides the time Harry and me, her brother and Billy Donovan did Alvin in the talent show, was the image of the crucifix. Everywhere I looked, in the classroom, the dining hall, the church, the rectory, were larger than life carved images of Christ nailed to the cross with bloody globs of blood at his wounds. And he hung there for you. We came in second in the talent show. We should have won, but Angela Valareli's father was in the army and was fighting in Vietnam. She came out and sang the words 'My father left for Vietnam/He'll be gone/for three whole years' to the tune of 'Greensleeves'. So she took first place even though we were the best act.

Dr Hale loves opera, especially Italian opera. He has thousands of records, tapes and CDs. There is no longer good opera in Boston he says so he goes to New York. One of the highlights of the many highlights of his year is when Dr Hale goes to New York City for the opera. For days after his return he is in a euphoric state, walking around the house as if on air, humming and singing to himself. I know nothing of opera. My music interests stopped abruptly when I was a teenager. Over the years, having heard various operas that Dr Hale has played on his stereo, and though I speak no Italian or German, one thing is for certain: the same things that happened to people then, happen to people now. I can tell by the highs and lows of the songs. Dr Hale says this is where they fall in love or this is where someone has been killed and I already know that from the music.

Days that Mrs Hale is particularly annoying, I am anxious to give my notice. I am afraid to let it go. I feel that I need something I can cling to. A series of memories to form a skeleton on which no dead flesh hangs. Clean folded laundry. Lemon-shiny wooden floors. Oil-soaped mahogany railings and buffed brass door knobs. A glass pane so clean you could put your fist through. Fresh linens and perfectly made beds that others sleep in. Scrubbed sparkling sink bowls bath tile and tubs. Disinfected toilets. New shelf linings and neat coffee tables. A burning whiff of ammonia.

A clean house isn't everything Harry said. We were talking about our mothers. I couldn't understand why she could think I was lucky to have my mother. But she said I was. Harry always liked my mother. I never gave it a second thought when she was around Mother more and more. I noticed it in a marked way after Mother moved out to her Clark Street place. Up until then, I imagined that one of the reasons she was at our house was me. But when Mother moved, Harry never came around Grandmother's house. She already quit school, and I was with Harry at school or I was with no one. The popular crowd, those blessed with the right looks and skills, the cheerleaders, pom-pom girls and the boys they hung around with horrified me. I never felt so self-conscious as when I had to walk through the dining hall, alone, past rows of tables seated with the popular kids.

Nonetheless, I managed to do well in school, despite my math and science deficiencies. As I finished the tenth grade, the guidance councilor suggested that I switch over from the business course to the college course. I never had thought of going to college up until that time. I was lost, as any girl my age, still trying to figure out what was going on with my body, and imagining I would meet a nice boy and get married and have a family like girls from Wilton always did. Young as I was perhaps I still believed I could right all that Mother made wrong. College was a way to one-up my mother in a way she could never accept. I started taking French class in the eleventh grade and whenever I was around her, I spoke French words and phrases much to her dishevelment. Speak English who wants to hear that crap no one can understand.

My father loved to fish. One of the few times he managed to get around Mother and take me somewhere we drove out on Route 133 where he parked his car on the side of the road. His fishing gear was in the trunk and we gathered it up and walked a winding woods path to a little pond. All the way to the pond he pointed out various things, like the difference between a hardwood forest and a softwood forest. How some kinds of trees grow leaves and shed them in the fall and other trees stay green all year long. I remember how the evergreen forest smelled like pine, different from the hardwoods which had a nutty aroma. Around the shallow edges of a cove, where the sun beat down on the muddy shore, a film of blue petroleum settled reflecting silvery blue and smelling like excrement. Father showed me how if the sun is out and you keep mind of your position to it, you can walk in a straight direction without a compass and you never have to worry about getting lost. He pointed to various kinds of birds, squirrels and chipmunks; and he knew the names of all the fish in the pond and what they ate. I felt sorry for the worm when it wriggled as he spiked it with the hook. But when my plastic red and white float started bobbing just like he said it would, I counted to five when it went under and set the hook. I was so excited I nearly fell in the water.

Somewhere in the trunk at the foot of the bed there's a photo he took of me holding my first and only bass. When we got back to his car that day, we discovered that someone threw a rock through the windshield. He brushed the broken glass off the seat very calmly and cleaned up the mess. While driving home he said it was unfortunate that there were some very mixed-up people in the world. But he assured me that mostly people were good, and he held my knee firmly in his right hand while driving with his left. Father didn't leave right after that. It may have been months or more. But that afternoon fishing is the last solid memory I have of being with him.

I wake and doze for several hours. A steady rain falls. Water rushes down the drainpipe from the roof to the spout outside my window and splashes on to the driveway. The heater is running less and less now. As spring approaches, as in fall, my room gets damp. I switch over from my panties and men's sleeveless white t-shirt to a sweatshirt and sweatpants. So I won't wake anyone in the middle of night with a whistling teapot, I boil my water in a tiny pan. Water spats scald against the inside of the pan. I steep the tea for a long time. I light a cigarette and draw deep. The menthol cuts cool into my lungs and I hold the smoke a second. Light hurts my eyes. During the daytime I wear sunglasses when I'm outside, I'm so frightened of making eye contact with anyone. I can do anything around the room in the dark like a blind person. I have no need to turn on the lights. Moreover, the stove pilot, electric digits on the clock, the red dot on the telephone machine and outside light spraying in around the drawn window shade deliver more than enough light for my eyes.

Fifteen

The tiny red light blinks fast. Her voice sounds desperate. Between sobs Denise says call me, you're the only person who I can talk to.

It could be anything with Denise. She loved to gather everyone around her hospital bed. Mother, Sully, Grandmother, me, her various boyfriends. When Mother was with Ray and they were going to take a trip to Las Vegas and leave us behind, Denise couldn't stand the thought of being left behind. I could see it coming and knew she was getting ready to cut. What she didn't expect was Mother would run off on vacation anyway. In the hospital, Denise acted out so badly they transferred her to a special unit at Bridgewater.

An orderly wheels me from my room to the room where they administer the ECT. It is often the same orderly who wheels me back, although at that particular moment, I'm unable to remember. The new combination of medications has completely eliminated my sexual urges. It's not that I'm active with anyone but myself. I feel like my feelings are filtered and slightly out of reach. Some of the drugs have a more distinct effect than others. I still find people attractive. Dr Isu. Dr Hale, though it took me years to see him that way. And there is a professional man about my age who is always on the seventy-seven bus, dressed smartly, reading a *Wall Street Journal*. He wears no wedding ring and I sit so I can watch him out the corner of my eye. The orderlies follow me around for days until my next treatment, making sure I don't wander off the unit. Maybe he can advise me what to do with my money.

Sometimes when I lay in the dark I hear Mrs Serge's piano notes. She plays many of the same pieces over again, and certain passages have become familiar to me. I don't know titles. Most of the authors have Russian names. She complains to me about the cook's radio which he keeps tuned loudly to a rock station, and when she plays the piano, he turns up the radio. She spoke to Mrs Hale about him and how he talks to himself; but Mrs Hale didn't seem to care.

Harry put up a fight. She clawed his face good. He had bite marks and several broken fingers. By the time the details got around Wilton, the citizens had twisted and inflated any factual detail. Nothing I heard would have surprised me. It was even said that she was the one who pulled the trigger to kill him with her last dying breath. Just take a little time off again, and just go out there again. Walk down the streets of the neighborhood, go to school. Have normal conversations with other kids. Denise later moved to Brockton and in with a boyfriend when she turned sixteen. A year later she left for California. In all those years since, I've only seen her once, and that was a time in between husbands, when she returned and lived briefly with me and Grandmother. Not long after that, she wound up in the hospital after another cutting incident. When she was released she moved back out west. It's been more than half a lifetime since she was regularly part of my life; it seems like yesterday, and she's as close as blood and a phone call.

All babies are beautiful one way or another.

Jennifer was the most beautiful baby I'd ever seen. More beautiful than Denise was as a baby. Jennifer got all of mother's looks. The blond hair. Turned up nose. Big round blue eyes so radiant it was hard to believe they were real. She was a gentle baby. Coos and caws when I comforted her. Happy little sighs. She always situated herself the same way when I fed her, with her delicate legs stretched out and crossed at the ankles, head back, gripping the bottle with her tiny hands, and, sometimes, I would let go just to see if she could hold it herself and it would tumble over out of her mouth. Before she crawled forward she crawled backwards, scampering around on Grandmother's living-room floor bumping into things. It never seemed to bother her being shuffled around from Mother's to Grandmother's and back. I wheeled her in the carriage and she smiled wide, the queen of the neighborhood.

In the new dream that I haven't dreamt yet, I'm standing on my father's grave somewhere in the hills of northern California. I don't know the name of the town. The sun is shining and the sky is clear and blue enough to scoop. The foliage is green, lush, the clean air smells of wild herbs and spices. I'm looking down at his grave, conversing with him. I still feel your hand on my knee. I'm sorry I didn't come sooner. My blood and my bones.

If you think something hard enough before you fall off to sleep you can shape your own dreams. When I was a girl, near Christmas, or the night before we went to Wahsburn Lake Park, I would think of nothing but Christmas morning, or riding the roller coaster with Harry. Sure enough during sleep that night I would dream of such events, though the dreams never turned out the way I'd hoped and I would miss the bus for the amusement park or Santa brought strange unusable gifts.

Denise had Mother's looks except for the black hair. Black Irish. My looks came from my father's family, Mother said they were all rolly polly and flat-footed. Once a month I cut my own hair. I've figured out a system using mirrors, holding one behind me and one in front of me. Nothing fancy, but I keep it short. Mrs Hale once asked me who cut my hair. I told her I cut it myself and she said oh. In my wilder days I grew it out full and long. Women said it was the kind of hair they would die for because it was so naturally thick and wavy. When the grays started coming, I dyed my hair various shades of red, brown, and even jet black. I tried jogging, working out at the gym, swimming. Once, for three months straight, I counted every single calorie and gram of fat I put in my body each day.

Harry broke her ankle playing basketball. Her leg was in a cast from the knee down for six weeks. She wore the first cast out in three weeks. Crutches she discarded the first day, they were too cumbersome and she found it easier hobbling on the stump at the bottom of the cast. Her wound couldn't slow her down. She played basketball, rode her bike and ran about with all her usual reckless energy. The doctor left her without a stump on the second cast, this forced her back on to the crutches because the break would never heal unless she gave it a chance. Even on crutches, Harry beat most boys at twenty-one on the basketball court.

The heater clicks on. It's only two or three times a night now. Soon I'll be sliding open the little window if I want some circulation. They grow everything in the yard. Tomatoes, greens, beans. There's a peach tree, a pear tree, and the grape arbor. Where they eat their ravenous meals, including the little girl who is only six or seven. She has beautiful long blond hair and blue eyes. It must have come from her father, because everyone on her mother's side is square-jawed and dark. They sit at the red and white check tableclothed picnic table to platters piled with grilled red meat, oversize salads, crusty bread and red wine by the gallon jug. On towards the end of summer and into early fall, the grapes ripen and air takes on a rich grape juice smell until the first frosts.

My mother always looked remarkable. I never saw her do anything close to exercising, though she always said eight hours running around serving drinks was all the exercise she needed. She drank, smoked, loved chocolate. I remember her sitting in bed, cigarette in one hand and a chocolate bar in the other, watching television. Her figure never changed.

I am walking out on the ice unsure of my footing. It is frigid, shades of gray. She is out there ahead, waving me on, far enough away that I can't see her face, only the slice of a figure and a waving arm. In her other arm baby Jennifer is wrapped in layers of blankets.

Mother continues to walk, cautious of the slippery ice despite my pleas for her to slow down and wait. The wind is blowing against me and my words go unheard. She is slipping and sliding as I am, she turns and waves me on again. Farther out on to the frozen lake she heads into a hard wind. My face and the edges around my ears are numbing over. The ice is beginning to swell, surge, and crack. Great blocks are separating from the main body of the frozen lake top. Mother and baby Jennifer become imprisoned on a floating block drifting rapidly away.

Sixteen

There are two calls from the same man waiting on the machine. This is a message for Laurel Bell. I am Dan Grassfield, your sister's husband. Please call me as soon as possible. There's been an emergency. The second message is exactly the same, except his voice sounds more grave.

The answering machine is on when I phone. I leave a message. I am Laurel Bell. I am returning your call. I brew tea, open a can of soup. Odor of fried fish. They cook fish every Friday. My soup is bland. I eat because I need nutrition. I smoke. I drink more tea. Eventually I slip from the tiny kitchenette chair and settle into bed with a fresh cup and pack of cigarettes but, before doing so, I turn the ringer back on the telephone in case he should call.

I'm startled, and I jump when the telephone rings, spilling tea on to the bed and losing my cigarette on the bed sheets. I recover my cigarette and answer the phone. It is Dan Grassfield. He hates to have to meet over the phone this way, and with such hard news. Denise lost the baby. The grief was so painful that she tried to kill herself. Judging by how he tells me the story, he knows nothing of Denise's history and as far as he knows, this is the first time. I wonder how you can be married to someone and not know the most basic things about them. But what can you learn when you marry someone you've only known for six weeks? Despite the fact that he dropped a wife and family for her, I almost pity him for his ignorance. He wants me to take a trip out there to try to help. He offers to pay for my flight. I assure him there's nothing I can do if I should fly out there; I am in a difficult situation of my own at the present time, and it would be nearly impossible for me to fly to California. He leaves me a phone number where I can reach her in the hospital. Please call her there. I know she wants to hear from you.

Several neighbors say they heard two quick pops in the night. Other than that, no one heard anything. The newspapers and television stations keyed in on the same image. A black body bag being lifted down the stairs on a stretcher. I was never sure whose body was in the bag. The alienation in the eyes of the four uniformed men who carried it down the stairs said it all. It was one of those photos, as soon as it became clear in the dark room, the photographer knew it was payday.

It's not too late for me to have a child. These days women regularly give birth right through their forties. I don't need a partner. At the sperm bank I could choose a donor from any background I wish. I'd select Mediterranean. Italian or Greek. Someone with some skills in the math and sciences to round things out. Maybe someone with a thin frame, small-boned. Perhaps it's for the best about Denise. Not that she cut again. That she lost the pregnancy. This is the first time I am aware that she's cut in several years. And what did she tell him about all her scars on her arms and legs. Those thin arms carrying her traumas in thin slivered marks from inside above her palms all the way up. And when she didn't cut she took pills while managing to phone someone at the last minute so she'd be rescued in the nick of time. How could he make love to her and not see the scars and not know what they meant.

I was jealous of how close Harry was getting with baby Jennifer. Whenever I went to pick Jennifer up, Harry was there playing with her. If Mother was supposed to come to Grandmother's for Jennifer, she sent Harry. Your mom's busy Harry said I'll take her back. However, somehow, I felt more at ease knowing that Jennifer was under the watchful eye of Harry rather than my mother.

Close the door and put the quarter in Harry says. I close the round glass door and the metal rim snaps shut. I hesitate. Put the quarter in she yells from inside the clothes dryer. Her voice is muffled and metally. I slip the coin through the slot and turn the little knob. The machine rolls into motion and Harry rolled up inside rotates around in three hundred and sixty degree turns. A wide grin's spread on her face as the machine twirls her at a dizzying pace. She tries to persuade me to try but I won't. We use all of our quarters to keep her spinning around in the dryer the entire length of the ten-fifteen mass.

I don't believe he meant to hurt anyone that

night. The pistol was out in the truck. He only went out for it later. There was an hour's time in between. Apparently he sat down and poured himself a drink. The baby never woke up. They say he drugged her. They say he drugged them all. They say that he drugged himself too. But he did have an hour, maybe as much as two. He sat there in the living-room chair with a drink. His face was scratched and bleeding and several of his fingers were broken.

The summer before I went into the eleventh grade's when factory row burned. It was a tremendous fire that went on for twenty-four hours. Flames and smoke were seen from as far away as New Bedford, Fall River and Rhode Island. Arson was suspected but there was never any conclusive finding. Every one of the old factories either burned to the ground or was gutted. Most of the buildings had long since been vacant; by the time I was a girl Wilton's shoe industry was a thing of the past. After the fire, police and firemen ribboned off most of the area which comprised of a dozen square blocks. Some of the old red brick walls were standing on make-shift staging and braces.

It was one of the rare days Harry and I were

together that summer. She was working at a dry cleaner's and recently quit or was fired. Things weren't going well at home so she was threatening to run again. We were too cool for riding bikes by that age, though neither of us drove, and we were hanging out in the center of town just walking from corner to corner. It was hot out and we debated whether we should spend the money for a bus home to get our swimsuits, and then go to Meadow Pond for a swim. Suddenly, she said I know let's go down and see the factories. What was there to see? I asked her. Besides, no one was allowed down there it was dangerous.

Several weeks had passed since the fire. A lot of the publicity had waned. There was still a police officer on each end of the street which was now roadblocked. To avoid the officers we walked down a side street, cut up through an alley, slipped under some yellow ribbon and we were inside the ruins. I was afraid and the entire area looked like it had been bombed. I couldn't find any sure footing underneath me and when I saw the brick walls leaning over into the braces I told Harry I wasn't going any farther. C'mon she said you'll never know what we might find, and she made her way around kicking through the rubble. I knew her well enough to know that the more I begged her to come back, the farther out into the danger zone she would go, so I kept quiet, walked back behind the ribbon and watched her. At one point she held up some shriveled and burned pairs of old shoes. What's your size. I said nothing, with my heart beating fast, expecting a wall at any moment to tumble and take Harry down with it.

Seventeen

I suddenly blank out. It seldom lasts longer than a few seconds and when I come around I'm not aware I've gone out. Like being woken up sharply from sleep, I open my eyes but my consciousness hasn't caught up with them yet.

It's happened while I'm riding on the bus. I miss a block and, on occasion, my stop. One time at the Hales' Mrs Hale brought me out of a blackout while I was standing in the middle of the living room with the vacuum cleaner in my hand, completely unaware of who or where I was. My biggest fear is that I will be outside and walk out into a car. Months can pass without such incidents; or it might happen twice in week. It was a good reason to stop driving.

An absolute whiteness until references in the environment slowly paint colors on to my blank memory. Your name is Laurel Bell. You are at the South Shore Medical Center and you have just had a treatment. Do you understand what I am saying?

The birds are returning. I hear them outside the window. They move through the yard at first light. Except for the few parks, trees are scarce in the city. But for some particular reason the backyards that come together at this point in the neighborhood are heavily treed and populated with birds. Now they are the tiny ones, chirping in a swarming chorus. The heat clicks on. There's still snow melting on the ground. I reach down and rub between the layers of fat on my belly. I bring my fingers to my nose and inhale the sweat.

Warm air reaches up to my toes, in soft currents it works its way up to my legs, mid-section, face and head. The tea is room temperature. I light a cigarette and draw. Two days since sleep. In air pockets knotty stomach stuff festers. Dust swirls and resettles according to the air-stream. Quivering shadows swim in exhaling smoke, elements of me in what is around me. Smoke returns in warm drafts. The heater abruptly stops. Birds again. Components of me settle in millions of particles. When I walk

through the door and down the hall they follow
me. They follow me into the bathroom. They
follow me into the dining room. They check on
me in the smoking lounge. The earth is wet
brown. The snow clings in shaded clumps,
dirty-white with black mascara.

Baby Jennifer should have slept at Grandmother's house. For some reason, at the last
moment, Mother picked her up, insisting that
she wanted a quiet evening off with the baby.
Usually on her nights off she didn't want
Jennifer because she had something going on at
the apartment or she and Ray went out. At that
time there was some kind of court order for Ray
to stay away from the apartment. Thinking
back, Harry was there when I was picking up or
dropping Jennifer off, but I surmise she must
have remained out of sight in one of the rooms.
Grandmother was just putting dinner on the
table. It was winter, Christmas vacation from
school. I was in the eleventh grade. The tree was
still up and all the new clothes and toys we
bought for Jennifer sat underneath the dying,
sagging branches. We sat down for dinner, me,
Denise and Grandmother. Baby Jennifer was in
the high chair. Mother stormed in and said that

she was going to take Jennifer for the night after all.

Big crows move in as the morning passes, chasing smaller birds away. They crow loud and long. The entrance to my apartment door is a half-door and I must stoop down. There is no hall or entranceway, I step directly down three wooden steps into the room. Forms come together, images and shapes correspond to each other. Then I take too much for granted, let my guard down and the lines and boundaries shift until there are gaps I can't account for. I lick it all and place it under my nose. Colors stain my tongue rancid greeny purple. The crows are crowing. Mother walks ahead of me, blanket-wrapped Jennifer in her arms. Wind is blowing hard across the open ice. There's not one surface of the place without blood on it. Water cannot wash it away. My ears are numb from the cold. I want the heater to come on but it is too warm. Blood spots the ice and snow drifts. The contents of my nostrils freeze and melt.

Eliza is a sickly child. Her nose runs continually and every week she has some kind of stomach virus or cold flu. She keeps Mrs Serge very busy between visits to the doctor's office and tending to her every need at home. Mrs Hale is around most of the time, but she takes no physical part of the day-to-day duties. Someone does the cooking. Someone does the cleaning. Someone takes care of her children. Regarding the children, Mrs Serge reports to Mrs Hale. If Mrs Serge isn't exactly clear, or didn't ask the doctor about a particular detail that Mrs Hale has deemed important, Mrs Hale shows great impatience with Mrs Serge. The same way she does with the cooks. The same way she does with me. Eliza is just beginning to stand and walk around holding herself up. The first time she did it, we called Mrs Hale into the room so that she could see but she was unresponsive.

Since she had Eliza, Mrs Hale spends more and more time sitting in the family room big chair watching television. She likes news shows, especially world news, and while watching, she invariably wears a panic-stricken look on her face. Whenever I pass by the room or come within ear-shot of her, she retells grim details of reports from the four corners of the earth. I don't know what this world is coming to is one of her favorite phrases. Then she spews out one sweeping statement like if they would only stop doing this or start doing that then the problem would immediately go away. When she's not in the big chair she sleeps. The kids are off to school on their own with the help of Mrs Serge. Mrs Hale rises mid-morning and takes Eliza until noon before her coffee and some toast. If time allows she naps in the afternoon. She's very shy about socializing even though Dr Hale has such a busy social calendar. I've frequently heard arguments between the two of them. Usually Mrs Hale is attempting to get out of an engagement at the last minute, one of her migraines or a sore throat. Just tell them I'm ill you're the one they want to see anyway.

In the paper it said that she'd once been arrested for prostitution. I didn't believe it. Grandmother wouldn't admit or deny it. She said only that it was years in the past and no one ever knew the truth about it except my mother. She did try to settle down with my father, and with Sully. She quit waitressing for a time during each marriage. She was never a housekeeper and was clueless to the ins and outs of running a household. She mixed whites and darks in the laundry, couldn't get a vacuum to work because she never changed the bag, cooked out of cans or we ate frozen dinners.

There was always plenty of beer. My father didn't drink more than a beer or two. It got to be another wedge between them when he learned that my mother often drank beer through the afternoon while watching television or sitting out by the pool. Even at work she drank and was fond of making jokes about her special cups of coffee. One too many gin and tonics her chin dropped and she began repeating herself in slurred words. Then she would instigate an argument with him and start getting rough. Once she punched him in the face. Another time she scratched his arms. He would just cover himself up to defend himself the best he could. For Christ's sake he said what about Laurel.

Eighteen

I walk up a long steep rocky slope. Rocks crumble under my feet. A wind blows from behind and lifts me with it. Mother's words echo in the air.

Laurel, don't let . . .

And then it trails off. Where are you? I cannot see her. There are clouds and mist blowing overhead.

Laurel, don't let . . .

And then it begins to drizzle drops of blood. Steadily it falls, harder and until the ground is blanketed and the air a red sheet. I hear Mother and call her. The blood is soaking my hair, seeping into my eyes, my clothes, down my neck and back. I continue to climb, my feet unsteady on the slippery ground. The slope becomes steeper until I am forced to use my hands to pull myself up. My palms are cutting on the sharp rocks. I am calling her. My blood is mixing with the raining blood.

Mother was a shoplifter fond of changing price tags. I was always frightened to death when she took me shopping. While waiting in line I wondered fearfully if her scam would be detected and we'd get arrested in front of everybody in the store. For years she bought clothes and groceries with her own markdown system. When I needed a new dress for junior-high graduation, we went to Lake's Department Store and found the beautiful dress that I wanted. Mother thought the dress too expensive, and switched tags with another dress which was marked down ridiculously low. When the cashier rang the dress she stopped and said she thought it was a mistake. They called the manager who said the dress was the higher price and someone must have changed the tag. Mother argued with him, the law said that the customer only had to pay what the merchandise was marked. In the end, the manager won. I think he knew that Mother changed the tag and, if it came to it, Mother would have to back down rather than stand accused. She turned to me at that point and said that's a lot of money do you still want the dress? Everything went quiet, all eyes were upon me, the manager, the cashier, Mother's, the other customers who were behind us in line. I looked at the dress, and I looked at Mother, who was waiting for an answer. Yes, I said, I do. Outside the store she acted as if the incident never happened and I doubt she gave it another thought. I wore the dress and went to the dance without a date. Harry was supposed to meet me and we would go together. But she appeared at the dance an hour late, very drunk. I walked home alone and was in bed by nine. I never wore the dress again.

Another one of her tricks was to have us eat candy bars and drink soda in the market while she was shopping. Denise became a rampant shoplifter for a while. She was caught twice. The first time she was young and they let her go. Later she practiced mother's switching tags technique. If she needed money she returned the merchandise claiming it was given to her for a gift without a sales slip, and received full price back. She did this at various stores around Wilton, then Brockton. And when they caught her she was prosecuted but pulled a suicide attempt before the trial date and ended up in the hospital. Eventually the incident was dismissed because of her mental health.

I called Mother's early the next morning. I wasn't expected to pick Jennifer up until around noon but knew if Mother and Ray were up late, Jennifer might need some tending. There was no answer. I waited a little while. There was no answer again. Sometimes Mother slept very soundly and I had to let the phone ring for a minute or more. Even if the ringer woke her up she could fall right back to sleep. I was afraid they were passed out and imagined baby Jennifer in her crib with a soiled diaper, hungry and crying.

It was a cold Saturday morning and there were tiny snow flakes spitting in the air. Foster Street was quiet. None of the kids were out yet. Cars were sitting quiet in driveways collecting snow. The wind whipped the trees and rattled the loose drain pipes and gutters on the rickety houses. Snow flakes blew harder, making a tick sound against my jacket. I turned down Curtis Street. In my head I was singing 'California Dreaming' which at that time was Denise's favorite song. She bought the record and played it over and over again. *On such a winter's day.*

Everywhere outside things are clanging and banging. Trash cans are overturned and rolling around on the ground. Loose windows are shaking in their frames. Screen doors are whipping open and snapping back. The rain has stopped, the wind is fierce. It is March. At first I gave myself until April and then moved it to May. To force myself into some other kind of situation. For two days it rained and now the wind. There have been no birds. I don't know where they go when it's windy and rains.

I smell fish. I hear screaming and banging. The grandmother shouts out the little one's name then yaps in rapid sentences. The mother gets involved with her own verbal assault which I can't be sure is aimed at her daughter, or mother, but she ends up crying. Finally the grandfather enters with his own brand of shouting and then it sounds like objects are being thrown.

Every hospital smells the same. That unmistakable sterility. One tiny whiff of it and I can be thrown into the cauldron. Spotless. Shiny. White. Shiny. Spotless and white. Bland food.

Friendly orderlies. Nurses you get to know and forget. You call them by their names, and the next day you can't remember. They wheel me down an elevator through a series of corridors into a room.

A light. A shadow. A voice.

I smoke in a room where they let the patients smoke and an orderly watches us through a window.

In order that I forget. In order that certain parts of my memory are temporarily burned out. In order that I start fresh. In order that I can be Laurel Bell. In order that I can be at the South Shore Medical Center. In order that I have just had a treatment. In order that I am meeting my orderly, or nurse, or another patient, for the first time. In order that they can follow me around in case I should wander off the unit. In order that I met him yesterday. In order that she was here last night but I don't remember.

It's been harder without Grandmother. She always knew when it was time. I no longer slept or got out of bed. I stopped eating and bathing and couldn't get up to go to the bathroom. She hated to do it. She would call and they would

come and take me and I would go without
word, Grandmother by my side in the ambu-
lance. Every time I came back she tried her
hardest to help. Let's make that the last time
you can do it if you really want.

All the kids stared and talked. Some walked
right up to me what was it really like in there?
Teachers acted as if they were afraid of me. I
was on medication. They gave me and Denise
tranquilizers to get us through the wake and
funeral. The doctor and Grandmother thought
we should stay on them for a little while. Denise
wouldn't go back to school. She cut herself
within days of the funeral said she didn't want
to live either.

It was more than the pot and drinking that
came between me and Harry. I think it disap-
pointed her that I wasn't that way. The trouble
with you is you won't let yourself go. That's
what she said the time we tried to do it and I got
so uncomfortable. If you'd only let yourself go
you might like it. And Harry started hanging
around with Annie Smith who was also known
as a tomboy and for a while they were insepara-
ble and I saw very little of Harry. Without
Harry my only friend was Billy Donovan who I

only saw if I went down the Curtis School where he hung out. He always tried to get me to go out more, and invited me to beer parties out in Bear Hill Reservation.

Nineteen

Ray's truck was parked in front. Mother smashed up the Cadillac. I don't know whose baby Jennifer was if she wasn't Ray's.

The snow was falling harder and everything was quiet. A car rolled slowly down the street. I could see headlights before I could hear tires rubbing over the newly fallen snow. It was Mr Harrington. He saw me and pulled over to the curb. Rolling down the window he said hi Laurel in his squirrely manner of speaking. He barely moved his lips when he talked, so it made it difficult to understand him. He raised his head and looked me straight in the eyes. Seen her? Have you seen her? I hadn't in days. He rolled up the window and drove on, the sound of his tires crunching the snow.

There have been no calls from Denise or her husband. Anything could have happened by now. He's flown her off to Paris for a second honeymoon. Or the marriage has been annulled. It isn't flying that scares me. You just give yourself over to it I imagine. When I was little and I flew to Florida, I was too excited to be scared. I'd have to buy tickets. Pack. I don't even own a suitcase. Get to the airport and find out where the plane is then be on a plane in close quarters with all those people only to land on the other side of the country in a city I've never seen before.

I knew about Harry and Peggy Rotondi. She was the park instructor. Every summer for the month of August, the city gave jobs to older kids, some of them in college. One boy and one girl per park. They came five days a week armed with bats, balls, basketballs and volleyballs purchased by the city. The stayed at the park from nine to four and organized games. In our park things were more crossed over than other parks, and the games were co-ed. Peggy and Martin were the coaches on each side and while the teams changed daily, Harry always ended up on Peggy's team. I thought when I saw them, close that way, touching and laughing with everyone else around, there was nothing to think. Then Harry began going off to lunch with her in the Mustang convertible that Peggy's father, who was a town selectman, bought her when she graduated high school. Peggy was pretty and wore make-up and didn't look like a tomboy. Lots of the boys had crushes on her. She was going to Bridgewater State College in the fall. I saw her and Harry on the grass. It was innocent enough. Harry was flat on her back and Peggy was leaning over her, tickling Harry's stomach and Harry was laughing helplessly.

Harry defended herself to the end. She fought him with every last trick. She bit, clawed, punched, kicked, gouged and pulled hair. But he managed to nail her with a decisive blow. They say he never meant to do it. His friends said he went there to make amends and one last effort to win her back. They followed me around. Some kids did. They said horrible things. Best we put all of that behind us. The police gave her information. About Ray. About my mother. They follow me around. I wander away. Sometimes the cramps can double me over.

I tried hard to stay off the medication during my natural period. I read books about herbs and nutrition. I took yoga classes and meditation. For nearly two years I didn't eat meat, fish, bleached white flour or processed sugar. I refused any notion of help from Western medicine. I took myself off my meds and stopped seeing my doctor who was prescribing them and the shock treatments. I began reading about Taoism and Buddhism. They were so contrary to everything I'd learned from Catholicism. There was no blood. No suffering on the cross. Only suffering through existence. And for a while I believed I found a way. I wore certain colors like purple and orange because I believed in their special powers.

Nancy could be cruel. We'd be having a nice moment, just hanging out together. Stop rubbing your hair she'd bark out. Or worse, you're sniffing again. She had a way of constantly reminding me of all my shortcomings. All the things that made me so self-conscious. If we were going out somewhere with her friends, I never had any, she often reminded me, she made sure to say don't touch your hair and don't blink. Blinking is another habit I picked up over the years. I can sit for hours, alone, and blink obsessively. You're a freak, she said in the end. Who would want to live with you?

The Harringtons eventually sold their house and moved. I tried living life again. I ran errands for Grandmother. I went to the movies and waited in lines next to everyone I know who knew. This is my home Grandmother said. I needed her; and in some ways, the more of a burden I was to her, the more it became obvious how much she needed me. The house was so small when I went back. After the men came and hauled a lifetime of accumulations away, the empty rooms seemed cloying, especially my bedroom of helpless years in bed, smaller than my tiny basement studio.

They say I wandered around in the snow storm for hours. It snowed heavier through the day. The biggest storm of the winter. Billy Donovan saw me in Wilton Center, and when he approached me I had a completely blank look in my eyes and wouldn't talk to him, it was as if I didn't know who he was. My hands were frozen, and he shook me and asked what was wrong. My first memory of Billy that day is sitting in the Pewter Pot Muffin Shop. We were at a booth and Billy ordered me coffee and I had already sipped half a cup. Still disconcerted, it was another half an hour before I was able to speak, and even then, the words only came one or two at a time and I couldn't complete a sentence. I don't think Billy believed me at first. He thought maybe I'd taken LSD and was freaking out. Eventually, as pieces of my story began to connect, he left me under the watch of the waitress and ran the two miles through the storm to Clark Street.

I rub my scalp, put my fingers to my nostrils and smell. Each part of my body, every tiny crevice, has its own particular smell. My scalp. The inside of my ears. My armpits. My feet, between my toes. My anus and my vagina. The inside corners of my eyes. So many smells. Aaron said it was called obsessive compulsive behavior. Under the circumstances, it wasn't unusual at all. We had as much control as we had no control over our actions he said. It was all right to be human. When he woke in the morning his eyes were bloodshot, he sat on the edge of the bed groaning, trying to keep himself from being sick. If he couldn't, he ran into the bathroom and vomited in the toilet. Aaron had a way of kneeling over the toilet like he was praying, groaning long painful groans in between. Then he would put some brandy in his coffee and go off to a twelve-hour work day.

Even my stomach has its own smell. Burning, acidic, decomposing. It's on my breath, I cup my hands over my mouth and nose, breathing out with my mouth and in with my nose. As the day goes on light forces its way through every possible crack. Every object in the room clarifies. A young girl was found dead on the side of the road. Her breasts were cut out. Her vagina was badly bruised. The corpse lay by a fence. Minute particles rise from my skin. I breath them back in. Some things can crumble in your hand. The tissue. The rioting of bitter tastes and smells. You look like the face on a coin, that's what a sweet crazy man I once met in the hospital said every time he saw me. I lose the light and assume the body of another, and become that other. She was sexually violated in every hole. The sound, the crows now. Unrelenting. Losing my footing. The ice beneath me cracks and she is no longer in front of me. I mustn't remain in bed. I need sleep. I am white and sterile. My hands and fingers tingle. I wriggle them to motion. Smoke a cigarette.

MY GROUND

They have great black wings. You cannot fall
off the world only through the ice.

Twenty

There are three messages. The first is another from Dr Hale. Laurel I'm beginning to grow concerned please phone me. Second is Denise's husband, call at my next possible convenience. Third is Dr Isu's voice inquiring about my missed appointment. I unplug the machine and the red light goes out.

Upstairs the little girl is crying. The adults are yelling. I don't know what day it is but it's dark. I didn't know what to make of it, what they said about Harry and Mother. They say he never went there to do anything but when he found them that way he went crazy. There is no reason to bathe. There is no reason to change my clothes or the bed sheets. Sometimes when the grandmother is downstairs in the basement doing laundry, she pauses by my door and listens. She knows I'm in here, but I am absolutely silent. She must smell the smoke. She stands there listening.

Black and minute glints of white. In California there are many colors. They told the story in the most sensational manner. Newspapers. Radio. Television. The same photo in the Wilton paper as in the Boston newspaper's front page. Those men carrying the body bag down the stairs in a stretcher, and on the television those few long seconds making their way down the stairs. Over and over for days. And the side stories and reporters calling and showing up at our door. Until the next catastrophe. And he hung for you. And they put spikes through his hands. A girl was found dead on the side of the road. Her breasts were cut out. Her vagina was badly bruised. And the photo of the rest area out on Route 133 where the body was dumped.

I try to eat soup but it tastes of metal. The door was slightly ajar but I didn't think anything of it. Bright Christmas colors. The first thing was the Christmas tree fell over. Bulbs broken all over the floor in the front room, strings of lights strewn everywhere still lit. Clean house clean mind. A watched pot never boils. Stay away from the woods there are bad men living there. Days go by I won't look directly at my skin. The dim shape of the telephone or glint of faucet over the sink. Hours count off second by second in my forehead. They said he was driven to madness by love. I experience abrupt pains in my skull, striking through to various nerve centers. I could be an attractive woman if I only lost a little weight and did something with my hair and dress.

She stands by my door and listens. She grills meats and sausages by the plateful. In spring she turns the soil in the garden herself, working the pick like a man, swinging it over her head, the blade cuts into the ground at intervals I can clock. The sound of hard metal strikes into soil and small rocks. I don't know what she expects to hear, what she conjectures that I do in here. There. He hit her. Now they're all screaming again. She was found naked. Her clothes were nowhere around. The men in the woods who could harm me. And they built Harry's house there. The men must have moved. Even with the windows shut I can smell the fat burning on the grill. Sister Agnes spread her hands out, tilted her head back, rolled her eyeballs into the upper sockets and stood there. But it's fish I smell. My earwax. I don't remember myself. Her breasts were cut out. They said it was some kind of Satan worship group. Sully said c'mon Laurel you know you want it. Sully sells seashells by the seashore. Don't say that. Just did. Not getting out of bed to go to the bathroom's when I know it's time Grandmother said. A light. A shadow. A voice. Darlings. Angels. Dear ones. The cramps are easing up, I am flowing.

She was living under the bulkhead. How long have you been there Harry she was cooking on a portable stove. Macaroni and cheese. Ray beat up his teacher in junior high. She had to go to the hospital. They sent him to reform school. They told my grandmother. She told me later. Before he moved here Ray beat up a policeman with a baseball bat and they sent him to jail. Ray sat at the table in the yard, shirt off, his muscular dark arms always at a slight flex even while holding a hand of cards. Denise bouncing on his knee. She lived under the bulkhead for sixteen years until the police came. Sixteen days. I am wet. I light a cigarette. My teacup is empty. The police brought her to Fall River. Or Brockton. The lights were still blinking all over the rug and the fallen tree. She's in California I haven't seen her. Wrapped wrists.

Harry knocked over the tree then passed out in the middle room. It was absolute quiet. She was on her stomach. You can smell it coming through the walls. And she carries it on big platters. Her eyes rolled up into the sockets. Breaking bulbs under my feet. The sound of them grinding into the rug. Blood dripping out from where the spikes were driven in. They never found her breasts. Or her clothes. They showed her mother and father on television. Harry what the fuck. She has no face. I turn her over she has no face. It's a mask but she has no face. I walked right past Ray on the floor in the front room next to the tree. I am wet. My hands are bloody. There is blood everywhere. All over Harry. All over the rugs and walls and the sofa. There is a crowbar next to Harry. It is coated with blood. I'm throwing up all over Harry. I see the crib and rise slowly like in a dream. Baby Jennifer is sound asleep. She has a hole in the middle of her forehead and her hands curled up above her shoulders.

The bedroom door is open. Mother's long legs are stretched out. They are covered in blood. The bed sheets are soaked in blood. Mother has no face either. I am sick again. I throw up on the floor. The smell of my vomit and the blood and the dead flesh and fish. It's coming through the cracks of the doors and windows. My hair is knotted from all the rubbing. The smell of my scalp is dried meat. I run out. Down the sidewalk my bootsoles leave red tracks in the white snow. I stop to fill my hands with snow and rub them red raw.